# Hiss-s-s-s!

# Hiss-s-s-s!

Eric A. Kimmel

Holiday House / New York

Library of Congress Cataloging-in-Publication Data

Kimmel, Eric A.
Hiss-s-s! / by Eric A. Kimmel. — 1st ed.
p. cm.
Summary: When a Muslim American boy named Omar finally convinces his
family that he should have a pet snake, it escapes and Omar learns why his
mother is so scared of them.
ISBN 978-0-8234-2415-3 (hardcover)
[1. Snakes as pets—Fiction.   2. Pets—Fiction.   3. Muslims—Fiction.]
I. Title.
PZ7.K5648Hi 2012
[Fic]—dc23
2012002968

*For Pirate*

# chapter 1

"I want a snake," Omar said. He could just as easily have said, "I want an elephant," or "Space aliens gave me a ride home from school in a flying saucer," and nobody would have paid any more attention. His family was sitting around the kitchen table. Mom and Dad were focused on the usual battle: getting Omar's little sister, Zara, to eat.

"I want Cheerios," Zara announced.

Mom rolled her eyes. She gave Dad her *You handle this* look.

Dad took over. He was much better in these situations than Mom. He had more patience. "Yes, I know, my darling," he said to Zara. "But Mom has prepared this wonderful dinner for us. There are eggplant and tabouleh and salad. All the things we love. It's all so good. How lucky we are to have a mom who loves us so much and feeds us so well."

Mom gave Omar a *Here we go again!* glance. Omar forced himself to look serious. Dad went through this routine just about every night and Zara still hadn't caught on.

"I want Cheerios!" she said again.

"Yes, I know, my love. But Cheerios are breakfast food. We don't have them at dinner. What we do have are eggplant and tabouleh and salad. It's all so good. I can't wait to eat it." Dad dug into his tabouleh with relish. "Yum, yum, yum!"

"Cheerios!" Zara insisted.

"Tabouleh. Yum!" said Dad. As he ate, he began telling a story. It was one of those ancient stories from Pakistan that must have been a thousand years old and that Omar had probably heard that many times. "Once upon a time, there was this crocodile who wanted to eat some monkeys for dinner. But monkeys are very smart. And they live high up in the trees. So the crocodile had to find a way to fool the monkeys to get them to come down from the treetops to the edge of the water so she could eat them. . . ."

As Dad told the story, he speared a piece of grilled eggplant on the end of his fork. He pretended that the eggplant was the monkey and he was the crocodile.

*Zap!* Goodbye, monkey!

Dad speared another piece of eggplant and started telling about the next monkey. After a few more eggplant monkeys, Zara said, "Let me do it. I want to be the crocodile."

"Okay," said Dad. He stuck another piece of eggplant on his fork. This time Crocodile Zara ate the monkey.

Omar had to hand it to Dad. The monkey story worked like a charm. By the time the last monkey figured out the crocodile's trick, Zara had cleaned Dad's plate.

"All gone!" said Zara.

"Hooray!" Dad said.

"Very good, sweetie!" said Mom. "What a big girl! Good job!" She passed Zara's plate to Dad so he could have his own dinner. "You're awesome. How do you do it?"

Dad shrugged. "Patience. Distract her. It works every time."

"I'm still impressed," said Mom as she rinsed off the plates and arranged them in the dishwasher.

Dad turned to Omar. "And speaking of patience, thank you for waiting."

"For what?" Omar asked.

"Weren't you trying to say something?" Everybody was staring at Omar now. It made him nervous.

"Oh, forget it," Omar said.

"No," said Mom. "Now is your turn, sweetie. Dad's right. You've been very patient. If there's something you want to tell us, say it. We're listening."

"Well...uh...okay." Omar took a deep breath. "I want a pet."

"All right. That's reasonable," said Dad. "What kind of pet do you want?"

"I want a snake," Omar said.

Dead silence. Zara giggled. "I want a monkey," she said. This time no one paid any attention.

"A snake?" said Dad. He sounded as if he didn't quite believe what he'd heard. "You mean...the animal? With no legs?" He wiggled his arm around as if he still hadn't grasped the idea.

"Yes," said Omar. "I'd like to have a snake. A pet snake. For a pet." He couldn't help repeating himself. Whenever he got nervous, words came tumbling out.

Mom looked up. She began waving her hands at the ceiling. "*Ya Allah!* Heaven give me strength! My family has gone crazy. Snakes! Monkeys! Crocodiles! What's next?"

"I want a giraffe!" Zara started yelling.

"That's enough!" Dad motioned for everyone to be silent. "Let's have some courtesy. And patience, please! Omar wants us to consider something, and no one is listening to him. That's not fair. Let Omar speak. We'll listen. Then we'll discuss."

"I've heard enough," Mom grumbled. All the same, she sat back down and waited for Omar to finish.

"Well?" said Dad. Several minutes of silence followed.

"I don't know what I'm supposed to say," Omar replied.

"Start at the beginning," Dad suggested. "Tell us why you want a snake."

"I want a rhinoceros!" Zara said. The word came out "rhinoskeros."

"Shhh!" said Mom. "Omar's talking."

3

"Sssssssss!" Zara hissed. "Ssssssssssssssnake!"

Omar waited for Zara to settle down. He had been practicing what he was going to say for the past week. He had fallen asleep the night before practicing his argument. Now was the time to put it to the test.

"You promised I could have a pet when I was old enough to take care of one. I think I'm old enough and I think I'm responsible. I get good grades in school. I keep my room clean. I do my chores without anyone reminding me. I babysit for Zara sometimes. If you trust me to take care of Zara, then I think I'm ready to take care of a pet. And the pet I want is a snake."

Mom shook her head. "No. No snakes. Not in this house."

"Why not?" Zara asked.

"Because I say so," Mom answered.

"Now, wait," said Dad. "We all need to learn more about this before we make a decision." He turned to Omar. "Tell me, son, what brought this on? What made you suddenly decide that you want to become a keeper of snakes?"

"I didn't suddenly decide, Dad. I've thought about it for a long time. I like snakes. I've done lots of research."

Omar began describing the advantages of having a pet snake. "Snakes make really good pets. They don't take up much room. They live in a habitat, which is like a fish tank, except its sides can be plastic instead of glass. Snakes are clean animals. They don't shed, so you don't have to worry if one of us might be allergic to them."

"Excuse me," Dad said. "You're wrong there. Snakes definitely do shed. They're reptiles. They shed their skins."

Omar sighed. Leave it to Dad to pick out a detail he'd overlooked. "That's different," Omar said. "The old skin stays in the habitat. You take it out and throw it away. It's not all over the house, like dog or cat hair. Some people are allergic to dogs or cats. Nobody's allergic to snakes."

Zara suddenly turned serious. "They could bite you. Then you die."

"That's not true, Zara," Dad said.

"Yes it is!" Zara insisted. "My friend Tony in day care told me."

"Your friend is wrong. Most snakes are not venomous. They don't have poison. They can't hurt people." Dad turned to Omar. "You weren't thinking of getting a cobra, were you?"

"I hope not!" said Mom.

Omar rolled his eyes. "No."

"Copperhead? Water moccasin? Black mamba?"

"No!" Omar said.

"Will it grow to be twenty feet long and swallow us while we're sleeping?" Mom asked. "I saw that documentary about those pythons in Florida. They started out as pets, too. Then they got loose in the Everglades. Now they're breeding like crazy and eating alligators and cattle. Tourists will be next."

"Mom, stop! Give me a break. I certainly am not getting an anaconda or a python, if that's what you're worried about," Omar said.

"What kind of snake do you have in mind?" Dad asked.

"A corn snake," Omar said.

"What's that? It eats corn?" said Mom.

Omar started talking fast. He wanted to get through this topic in a hurry. "No, they don't eat corn. No snake does. Corn snakes are carnivores. They eat meat. I downloaded a lot of information about corn snakes from the Internet. I have a whole file on my computer. I'll print it out if you like."

"Just tell us. Why a . . . corn snake?" Dad said.

"Everybody online says a corn snake is a good snake for a beginner," Omar said. "They're friendly. They like being handled. They don't get too big. They're good eaters. Some snakes can be really picky about their food."

"Good eaters?" Mom paused. "What exactly do these good eaters eat?"

Busted! Omar whispered the answer. "Uh . . . mice."

"Mice!" Mom shrieked. "Oh, no! End of discussion! I won't have mice in my house."

"I want a mouse, too," Zara said. "And a snake. And a rhinoskeros."

"How about fish?" Mom pleaded. "What's wrong with fish? I like fish. They're soothing."

"And a fish," said Zara.

Omar looked to his dad for help. Dad raised his eyebrows and stared back at Omar. *If you want a snake, you'll have to convince your mother.*

Omar wondered whether anything he could say would convince his mom. This was his one chance. It was the one argument he had to win.

"Mom, I can understand why you're upset. Corn snakes do eat mice. That's their food. They got their name because they hung around barns where farmers stored corn. That's where the mice were. That's why they're also called rat snakes." Oops! Omar saw his mother beginning to mouth the word "rats!" He hurried on.

"I know you hate mice. But it may not be as bad as you think. Snakes don't have to eat live mice."

"What do they eat, then?" Mom demanded. "Dead ones?"

"Uh...yeah!"

Mom gasped. "Omar, you can't be serious! Dead mice? In our refrigerator? Next to the food we eat? How can you even suggest something so disgusting? Never! Not in my house! Not while I'm the mom here!"

"Your mother has a good point," Dad said to Omar when Mom finished talking. "I don't want mice in our refrigerator, either. What do you say to that?"

"Can I have ice cream?" Zara asked.

"Later," Mom said. "We need to listen. Omar's talking." She turned to Omar. "Well?"

"It's not what you think," Omar began. "I've researched this. The mice are frozen. I can get them one by one at the pet store, as I need them. They will never be in the refrigerator. They will never be anywhere in the house except the snake's habitat. The snake will eat them quickly."

Omar hoped that was true. The snakes on the YouTube videos he'd watched gobbled down their mice in a couple of minutes. Omar had never actually fed a snake or watched a real one eat. He had no idea how long it took.

Mom kept her eyes fixed on Omar as he spoke. She waited until he finished. Then she sighed and quietly said, "You don't really want a snake—do you? Tell me you're joking. Please!"

"No, Mom," Omar said. "I'm not joking. I'm serious. I really, really want a pet snake."

That was when Omar realized he had won. By asking him that question, Mom had allowed him a little space. No more than a crack, really. But it was a crack wide enough for a snake to crawl through.

Mom turned to Dad. "If there's going to be a snake in this house, there have to be rules."

"I agree," said Dad. He took a legal-size notepad from the kitchen drawer and uncapped his big Mont Blanc fountain pen. It was the one he used at the office for signing important documents. "I think we can negotiate a compromise here," he said. "Omar may have a pet snake if he really wants one. But we all must agree about the rules." He turned to Mom. "Is that acceptable to you, Hoda?"

"Do I have a choice?"

"Yes, you do," Dad said. "If you really object to having a snake in the house, say so. Omar will have to come up with another pet."

Mom glared at Omar. Omar watched the clock on the wall. Two minutes passed. Finally, Mom let out a deep breath. "Okay."

"And you?" Dad turned to Omar.

"I agree," Omar said. "Thank you, Mom." He struggled to hold back his excitement.

"Don't thank me yet," said Mom. "I must be out of my mind."

"Can I have ice cream?" Zara asked again.

"Soon," said Dad. "We'll all have ice cream after we finish our business. Now, since we have all agreed to agree, let's write down what we're agreeing to." Dad wrote "1" on the pad in thick blue ink and began. He read the words aloud as he wrote them.

1. Omar will be fully responsible for the snake's care and feeding.
2. The snake will remain in Omar's room and will not be brought into any other part of the house for any reason.
3. No rodents, dead or otherwise, will be kept anywhere in the house except in Omar's room, inside the snake.
4. Should Omar no longer wish to care for his snake, he is responsible for finding it a suitable new home.

Dad crossed the last "t" and inserted the last period. "Does anyone wish to add anything else?"

"I do," Mom said. "Write this down. Omar is fully responsible for vacuuming, making his bed, putting away his clothes, and keeping his room neat and clean according to MY standards. Because as long as he has a snake in his room, I am not going in there."

Dad looked at Omar. "Agree?"

Omar had expected that. However, he already knew how to vacuum and how to sort, wash, and iron his clothes. He kept his room clean. Most of the time, anyway. So what he conceded wasn't really such a big deal. "Agreed," he said.

Dad added "5" to the list and wrote down what Mom and Omar had just agreed on. "Anything else?"

Mom looked at Omar. Omar looked at Mom. Together they looked at Dad. "No," they both said at once.

"Then we have a family agreement. All parties must sign." Dad held out the pen. Mom signed with loops and curlicues, as if she were writing her best Arabic calligraphy.

*Hoda Choufik-Kassar*

Omar wasn't used to writing with a fountain pen. He smudged some of the letters. The others were wobbly but readable.

*Omar Choufik-Kassar*

Dad signed next. Simple and businesslike.

*Ahmad Choufik-Kassar*

"Now me!" said Zara, reaching for the pen. She didn't quite know how to write all the letters yet. Dad guided her hand.

*Z A R A*

Dad tore the page off the pad. "I'll make four copies," he said. "One for each of us, and one to post on the refrigerator door so we can refer to it if there's ever a question."

"One for me! Don't forget!" Zara held out her hands.

"She can't read!" Omar said.

"We'll read it to her," Dad said. "I'll make five copies."

"One for Mommy. One for Daddy. One for Omar. One for me." Zara counted the copies on her fingers. "And one for the 'frigerator. Where the mice are."

"NOT!" Mom cried. She tried to look stern, but Omar could tell it wasn't working. He had carried it off.

*I did it!* Omar felt dazed. *I'm going to get a snake.*

Now for the next challenge.

*Where do I get one?*

# chapter 2

Omar was wrong. He realized that as he lay awake in bed that night, long after everyone else in the house had gone to sleep. The next question wasn't "Where do I get a snake?" It was "Where do I put a snake?"

A snake needed a home, especially if it was supposed to stay in Omar's room. At the moment, all he had to offer was drawer space.

At school the next day, Ms. Ortiz—aka the Big O—was reviewing fractions. Fractions were important because they would be on THE BIG TEST. The whole fourth grade had spent the past month getting ready for THE BIG TEST. Ms. Ortiz told them at least three times a day how important THE BIG TEST was.

Omar didn't get it. It wasn't like *American Idol*, where the winners won recording contracts and went on to become superstars. It was more like *The Biggest Loser*, where the goal was not to make a fool of yourself, like gaining ten pounds after you'd spent the whole week exercising. Getting a high score on THE BIG TEST didn't matter. The goal was not to flunk, because if too many kids flunked THE BIG TEST, the teachers would lose their jobs and the school would be closed down. At least, that was how the Big O explained it.

Omar didn't think that was much of a threat. What they should really do was give the kids the day off and have the teachers come in to take the test. Omar wondered why no one ever thought of that.

The Big O droned on and on. Omar tried to pay attention, but his mind kept drifting away. His thoughts wandered back to all the articles about snakes he had found on the Web. To successfully keep a snake as a pet, Omar would need...

He picked up his pencil and began making a list on his fractions page.

### 1. Habitat

This was where the snake would live. It could be an aquarium, but there had to be some way of locking the lid in place. All the articles said corn snakes were escape artists. They could go through any opening they could fit their head through.

### 2. Heat Source

Critical! Omar double-underlined the two words. Snakes, like all reptiles, are cold-blooded. They warm up by going to a warm place and cool off by moving to a cooler one. Since his snake couldn't get out of its habitat—hopefully—Omar had to make sure it could control its body temperature.

Most of the articles recommended a heat mat that fit under one-third of the habitat. That gave the habitat a warm side and a cool side. The snake could move around until it found the most comfortable spot.

### 3. Substrate

This was the bedding at the bottom of the cage. Ordinary newspaper would do. So would paper towels. If Omar wanted to get fancy, he could use wood shavings. But they had to be aspen. Pine and cedar had oils that were harmful to snakes. It all depended on how much money he wanted to spend. Omar didn't want to spend any money if he didn't have to. Newspaper was probably the way to go.

### 4. Water Dish

Snakes need fresh, clean water. They drink it. If they get too hot, they soak in it. Sometimes they pee and poop in it, some of the articles said. Omar would have to be prepared to change the water at least once a day, maybe more if it looked dirty. The water dish had to be big enough for the snake to soak in and heavy enough so it couldn't be turned over. Snakes like to rearrange their habitat.

Omar wondered if his mom had a bowl or dish that she'd let him use. On second thought, better not to even ask.

### 5. Somewhere to Hide

This was important. Omar underlined it, too. Snakes don't like to be out in the open, especially after they've eaten or when they're preparing to shed their skin. They need a place to hide when they don't feel secure. One article showed a water dish with a space underneath where a snake could hide. An empty toilet paper roll would also work. So would an empty cereal box with holes cut in it. Omar decided to start with a toilet paper tube. With four people in his family, he'd never run short of toilet paper tubes. Or cereal boxes.

### 6. *Food*

Omar underlined the word and put stars around it. Corn snakes eat mice, live or frozen. This was the key question. Where could he get mice? Omar had no answer. He knew he'd have to come up with one before he got his snake. No mice, no snake. It was that simple.

"It's that simple!" Ms. Ortiz said, repeating the words in Omar's brain. "Two-eighths is the equivalent of what? Omar."

"Huh?" Two-eighths could have been the equivalent of green Jell-O. Omar's thoughts wriggled around like snakes as he tried to come up with an answer. "Ummm...ummm...well, uh...umm..." He did recall that the Big O had been talking about fractions. He blurted out the first fraction that popped into his head.

"Five-sixteenths?"

The disgusted smirk that slithered across the Big O's face told Omar he hadn't even come close. "Wake up, Omar!" Ms. Ortiz said. Omar tried to look sheepish, but in his mind he saw a picture of Ms. Ortiz being swallowed by a gigantic anaconda. *Omar, help me!* she screamed. As he walked on by, Omar noticed that the snake had swallowed about five-sixteenths of her.

"One-fourth!" Ms. Ortiz wrote the fraction on the board. "One-quarter! Did you hear that, Omar? I expect one hundred percent attention. Not fifty. Not twenty-five. What are the fractional equivalents? Class!"

"One-half. One-quarter," the rest of the class sang out. Omar melted into his seat.

"One-half. One-quarter," he murmured, a second too late.

"Pay attention next time. I'll be calling on you." Ms. Ortiz fixed Omar with an unblinking snake stare before moving on to her next victim. Omar sat as still as a frozen mouse.

"Hey, guy! You sure stirred up the Big O," Samkatt whispered. Samkatt sat across the aisle from Omar. He was one odd kid, probably the oddest kid Omar had ever met.

For starters, his name wasn't Sam or Katt or Sam Katz. It was Philip, and he was Chinese. Samkatt was short for Samurai Cat. Philip—Samkatt—was obsessed with Japanese manga and anime, especially a series called "Fighting Teenage Samurai

Cats." When the Big O wasn't on his case, he filled the pages of his notebook and everything else he could find to sketch on with drawings of Japanese cats in samurai armor carving each other up with samurai weapons.

Omar thought Samkatt was a really good artist, especially when it came to drawing samurai cats. He hardly ever drew anything else.

Samkatt looked up from his drawing of one samurai cat lopping off another's arm. He glanced over at Omar. "What's all that stuff you're writing? It's not fractions."

"I'm getting a snake," Omar whispered back. "I'm making a list of what I need."

"Cool! I'd love to have a snake. But I can't," Samkatt said.

"Why not?"

"'Cause my parents don't 'get' pets. Why keep an animal around that you can't eat and that doesn't do anything? They don't 'get' my drawing, either. They think I should study more so I can be a doctor. Can you see me as a doctor?" Samkatt said.

*Maybe*, Omar thought. Samkatt could be a samurai doctor who operated with a sword. *Whoosh! Out comes the liver!*

"Can I see your list?" Samkatt asked.

"Watch out. The Big O's looking." Omar slipped his list across the aisle to Samkatt just as Ms. Ortiz glanced their way. He began copying fraction problems from the chalkboard as if it were his favorite thing to do.

Samkatt copied and solved the same problems in a few seconds. That was another peculiar thing about him. Right answers seemed to pop into his brain. He'd be drawing a samurai cat with its head cut off. The Big O would call on him with some question out of the blue and he'd answer it.

Omar tried to figure out how to take five-eighths from fifteen-sixteenths while Samkatt pored over Omar's snake supply list. "Did you buy this stuff already?"

"No," Omar whispered back.

"Good. Because I think I know where you can get most of it."

"Where?"

"Watch out. The Big O's on patrol," Samkatt said. He passed the list back to Omar, who slipped it into his notebook. Samkatt glanced at Omar's fractions. "Number eight. You're wrong. It's not three-fifths. The answer's five-eighths."

"Thanks," Omar said, erasing the numbers.

"No problem. Just let me play with your snake when you get it. What are you doing after school?"

"Nothing. Why?"

"Come home with me. There's this kid on my street who used to have a snake. He still has all the stuff in his garage. Let's ask him if he wants to sell. How much money do you have on you?"

"Eight bucks. Maybe," Omar said. "I haven't counted it."

"That's not much to work with," Samkatt said. "Okay, we'll see what we can do."

"Omar! Number eight!" The Big O's voice boomed across the room.

"Five-eighths, Ms. Ortiz," Omar said. The Big O didn't say anything, which meant that he—or rather Samkatt—had the right answer. Omar felt like a lucky little mouse who had just gotten away from a large, hungry snake.

# chapter 3

Omar and Samkatt walked home together. Omar stopped at the corner to readjust the shoulder straps of his backpack. The pack weighed nearly as much as he did. Lugging books back and forth to school had been a conscious part of Omar's campaign to get a snake. He had printed out a quote that he found on the Web and stapled it on the bulletin board above his desk.

IT'S NOT THAT I'M SO SMART. IT'S JUST THAT I STAY
WITH PROBLEMS LONGER.

The quote was from Albert Einstein. Omar liked thinking that he had something in common with the great scientist. Dad was impressed. So was Mom. Omar wondered if Albert Einstein's parents let him have a pet snake. Did scientists have pets? Or did they just take care of lab animals? Omar didn't know. What he did know was that, so far, everything appeared to be working. The downside was hauling all those books back and forth.

Samkatt cruised along on his skateboard. Samkatt didn't believe in backpacks. He hardly ever carried anything that wouldn't fit in his pocket. Samkatt didn't believe in homework, either. Omar had never seen him do any. Yet somehow, Samkatt always had his homework ready to be turned in and had always earned As when it came back. Omar was glad Samkatt was his friend. Otherwise, he'd probably hate him.

They went past the park and turned right by the gas station. Omar hulked along, lugging his backpack. Samkatt skated around him in lazy circles and figure eights. The little shopping malls and older homes gave way to newer developments. They turned left into the first one—Mountainview Terrace—and wound their way along the curving streets to the cul-de-sac where Samkatt lived.

Samkatt's house was the third of six houses built around a circular glob of asphalt. All the houses looked the same. They had beige stucco walls, steep roofs, postage-stamp lawns, and huge garages with wide driveways leading down to the street. A ratty-looking middle school kid wearing a stocking cap pulled over his ears and a faded Nirvana T-shirt rode a skateboard down the fifth house's driveway toward a wooden jump at the edge of the curb.

Omar could see at a glance what the kid was trying to do: gain speed and momentum coming down the driveway, hit the jump, grab air, then turn around and land in the street facing back up the driveway, ready to do it again. The idea was good. The kid just wasn't up to it. Omar saw that in the first jump.

The kid didn't have the confidence. He was scared of landing on his butt. Consequently, he held back when he hit the jump. He didn't gain enough height to make the turn. Down he went, flat on his butt on the asphalt. Omar remembered something his dad had once told him: Either you ride your fear or it rides you. Good advice for skateboarders. And snake handlers.

Samkatt skated over to help the kid up. "You okay?" Omar heard him ask.

The kid shook his head. "Caught my wheel somehow," he said.

Yeah, right! Omar set his pack down on the sidewalk. "You almost had it," he said.

"Yeah," the kid answered. "I can do jumps most of the time. Something's wrong with my board. I need to check the wheels."

"Yeah," Samkatt said.

"Yeah," said Omar.

Samkatt made the introductions. "Ray, this is my friend Omar. Omar, Ray."

"Yeah," Ray said, bumping knuckles with Omar.

"Ray lives next door. He goes to Farragut." That was the middle school where Samkatt and Omar would go in a couple of years. Omar guessed that Ray was close to thirteen, if he wasn't already. "I brought Omar over to meet you. You guys need to talk."

"'Bout what?" Ray asked. He pulled his stocking cap farther down over his ears. Omar could see the faint shadow of a middle school mustache on his upper lip.

"Samkatt told me you used to have a snake," Omar said.

"Yeah. Used to," said Ray.

"What happened to it?" Omar asked.

Ray shrugged. "It died. I still have the stuff."

"Can I see it?" Omar said. "I'm getting a snake, but I don't have stuff for it."

"He wants to know if you'd like to sell your stuff," Samkatt said.

"Maybe," Ray said. "How much you offering?"

"I need to see it first," said Omar.

Omar and Samkatt followed Ray up the driveway and around the garage. They entered through a side door. Ray flicked on the overhead light. Rows of shelving lined the garage walls. Two mountain bikes hung by their front wheels from hooks on the ceiling. A riding mower filled one corner. Why would anyone need a riding mower for a lawn that was only a little bigger than a blanket? Where was the snake stuff? Omar finally saw it on one of the shelves, half-hidden by a plastic storage box and a bag of potting soil.

"Is that it?" he asked. Ray nodded.

Omar crossed the garage to have a look. Not too bad. He added up the pluses and minuses. This was a real reptile habitat, not a converted fish tank. The lid slid into a frame that completely closed the top. No holes for a snake to get through. The lid's mesh was metal screening, sturdy enough so it couldn't be pushed out. No holes in the mesh, either. A hasp on one side allowed the lid to be locked down. Omar examined the sides. The glass was in good shape. Nothing cracked or broken.

He lifted the lid. A layer of wood shavings covered the bottom. Omar couldn't smell pine or cedar, so he guessed they were aspen. A heavy ceramic bowl rested in the far left corner. Water dish. Good. Omar still didn't see anything that might be a hide.

"What did you use for a hide?" he asked Ray.

"Huh?" Ray answered. Not good. Ray didn't even know what a hide was. "The snake liked to dig in the aspen. That's where he hid. Same thing, I guess."

*No, not the same thing at all,* Omar thought. He looked around for a heat source. "What did you do for heat?" he asked Ray.

"I had a lamp. It sat on top of the lid," Ray said. "The snake would sit under the lamp to get warm."

"Did you turn it off at night?" Omar asked.

"Yeah," Ray said. "I kept the tank in my room. The light kept me up."

"Uh-huh." No heat for the snake at night when the temperature dropped. Omar felt himself getting annoyed. Ray hadn't bothered to learn the first thing about what a snake needed. And the poor snake had to suffer for it. Payback time. Omar was going to take the habitat and all the equipment that came with it off Ray's hands to make sure that owning a snake would never cross Ray's mind again. And he wasn't going to pay more than five bucks.

"What do you think?" Samkatt whispered to Omar.

"Hate to tell you this," Omar said, taking Samkatt aside, "but your buddy Ray is a doofus. He doesn't know anything about snakes."

"That's no surprise," Samkatt said. "How about the setup? Can you use it?"

"Yeah. It's a good start. I can build on it."

"I'll find out how much he wants," said Samkatt.

"No," said Omar. "Leave it to me. I'll do the bargaining." Bargaining was something Omar knew how to do. His mom had taught him. If there had been Olympic medals for bargaining, Mom would have won the gold. Even in the snootiest department stores, where salesclerks wouldn't take so much as a penny off the price, she still came away with coupons, perfume samples, and tickets to special sales and shopping events.

The first rule, she had taught Omar, was never to admire anything. Be ready to walk away.

"Thanks for letting us see it," Omar said to Ray. He turned to Samkatt. "Let's go."

"You don't want it?" Ray said. "You told me you're getting a snake. You need a place for it."

"I do," said Omar. "But you don't have what I'm looking for."

"What are you looking for?" Ray asked. Aha! Omar had him hooked. Now he had to play him. Second rule: Criticize.

"I need something bigger," Omar said. "And a heat lamp is not going to cut it. I was hoping you had a heat mat on the bottom of the tank."

"Heat mat? I have one of those," Ray said.

"Where?" Omar asked, genuinely surprised. "It's not on the tank. I don't see any cord."

"It's in the box. On the shelf." Ray pointed to the cardboard box next to the snake habitat.

"Why didn't you stick it on?" Omar asked.

"Never got around to it," said Ray. "The lamp worked okay. You can have the heat mat, too, if that's what you want. With the lamp."

*Yes!* Omar thought. Now for the kill. "How much are you asking? For the whole setup. As is."

The answer came fast. Ray was eager to sell. Too eager. "Thirty bucks."

Omar turned to Samkatt. He shook his head.

"You ready?" Samkatt said.

"Yeah," said Omar. "Let's go."

"Wait!" Ray blocked the garage doorway. He didn't want them to leave. Omar almost had him in his pocket. *Easy....Be patient....Don't push too hard.* He could hear Mom's voice whispering in his ear.

"I'll make you a good deal," said Ray.

"How good?" Omar said.

Ray sucked on his lower lip. Omar could see the muscles in his jaw working as he tried to come up with a number. "Fifteen bucks. For everything."

Omar turned to Samkatt. "Let's go."

Ray didn't move from the doorway. "You're not leaving? Fifteen bucks is a good deal. You'll pay way more than that at PetSmart for all this stuff. Look!" He pulled the heat mat out of the box. It still had the price tag on it. "Just the heating pad is worth more than that. Twenty-five bucks! Look!"

Omar looked at the sticker, then at Ray. "It's not what I want. But if you'll take five bucks, we have a deal."

"Five bucks!" Ray slammed his fist against the Sheetrock garage wall. Omar wasn't impressed. Ray had probably seen that in a video. Tough guy, punching his fist through the wall. Except Ray wouldn't fully commit himself, just like on the skateboard jump. He didn't make a dent in the Sheetrock. But he did start yelling.

"I can get fifty bucks on Craigslist. At least!"

"I'm not stopping you," said Omar. "It's your stuff. You can do what you want with it. I just want to look around a little more. Let's go, Samkatt."

"Yeah. See ya, Ray!" Samkatt said. He followed Omar to the side door. The boys walked around Ray as if he were just another piece of clutter in the crowded garage.

"Wait!" Ray's jaw muscles were working. "Five bucks. You got it on you?"

Omar nodded.

"Deal," said Ray.

"Deal," Omar repeated.

They bumped to make it official. Omar took the lone five-dollar bill out of his wallet and handed it to Ray. Ray glanced down as if checking to see that it truly was a five, then shoved it into his pocket. He and Samkatt packed the heat lamp, the heat mat, and a half-full sack of aspen shavings into the habitat. Samkatt and Omar carried it out of the garage and set it in the driveway. Ray resumed practicing his skateboard jumps.

"You need help carrying that home?" Samkatt asked. "I can go with you. I'm not doing anything."

"Thanks," said Omar. "It's not heavy. Just hard to carry when I'm lugging my backpack."

"I have an idea," Samkatt said. He ran across the cul-de-sac to his garage. He came back with a Radio Flyer wagon. "It was my wagon when I was a kid," he said. "My mom still uses it for hauling stuff around."

"Cool!" Omar said. He loaded the habitat and his backpack into the wagon. "Thanks, Ray!" he called as he and Samkatt headed out of the cul-de-sac toward his house.

Ray didn't answer. He was still trying to make that jump.

# chapter 4

It took Omar and Samkatt only twenty minutes to get to Omar's house. Omar saw his mom's Prius in the driveway. Uh-oh! She was home. Omar hoped she wouldn't raise a fuss when he and Samkatt brought the habitat inside. The best way for that to happen was to make sure she didn't know about it.

"Let's be real quiet so I can get the habitat to my room before Mom finds out," Omar said as he unlocked the front door. Samkatt held the habitat. Even with all the gear inside, it was light enough for one person to carry.

"Dude, she's gonna find out anyway," Samkatt said. "May as well be now."

"You don't know my mom," Omar said.

"I DO know your mom," Samkatt said. "If you think an empty aquarium is gonna freak her out, what do you expect's gonna happen when you bring a live snake home?"

Omar had to admit that Samkatt had a point. Even so, he didn't want to see his mom getting stirred up again. "Just try to hold it down, will you?" he said.

"Yeah, yeah," Samkatt replied, maneuvering the habitat through the living room and up the stairs. The door to Mom's studio was the first one on the left when they got to the second floor.

When the studio door was shut, it meant that Omar's mom was concentrating on an art project and didn't want to be disturbed. When it was open—even just a crack—it meant that anyone could come in and visit. Omar usually looked forward to seeing the door open. He liked sitting in the studio, watching his mom draw and paint. Sometimes she used him as a model. Omar enjoyed that, even though it meant sitting perfectly still for a long time.

But today—just today—Omar really wanted to find the studio door closed.

So of course—wouldn't you know?—it was half-open. Omar motioned to Samkatt to be quiet. If they could just tiptoe down the hallway to Omar's room and get the habitat inside without Mom being any the wiser...but of course, "Samkatt" and "quiet" were total opposites. With a thump, Samkatt dropped the habitat on the hallway carpet right in front of the studio door and said, "Getting that sucker up the stairs was harder than I thought!"

"Omar? Is that you? Who's with you?"

"Samkatt, Mom!" Omar called back. "We just got home."

The studio door opened the rest of the way. Mom had on her work clothes: an old red flannel shirt over blue jeans, with a faded paisley scarf tied around her hair. The room smelled of oil paint and turpentine. Omar loved those smells. He had grown up with them. Mom had even taught him how to size a canvas to get it ready for painting. Not many kids had that skill. Omar felt proud that Mom trusted him enough to let him help her prepare the canvases she was going to paint on.

Mom had been spending a lot of time in the studio this year. She'd had two shows in galleries in Portland and had another one coming up in Seattle. The Seattle Art Museum had bought two of her paintings. She'd gotten calls from galleries in San Francisco and Vancouver, Canada, expressing an interest in arranging shows there. *Oregon Art Beat* had included her in a broadcast on northwestern artists. An art critic on the show said her paintings recalled those of a famous artist, Gustav Klimt.

Mom had showed Omar some of Klimt's paintings in an art book she'd had since college. Omar thought they looked weird. Mom didn't.

"Being compared to Gustav Klimt is a very big deal!"

For the past several months, Mom had been working on a series of paintings called "Dreaming in Arabic." She used a lot of Middle Eastern patterns and textures from scraps of old carpets and other textiles that she collected, along with bits of poetry, which she painted in flowing Arabic script. Today's work must have gone well. Mom appeared to be in a good mood. Hoping to keep her that way, Omar stepped in front of the habitat. Maybe she wouldn't notice.

"Hello, Philip," Mom said to Samkatt. Omar's mom was the last person on earth other than the Big O who still called Samkatt by his proper name. Even his parents had finally given in and called him Samkatt. But Omar's mom had never been known to care about what anyone else did. Philip was a perfectly good name and Samkatt a perfectly silly one. As she often told Omar, she saw no reason to indulge juvenile behavior.

She looked into the hallway. "What's that?" she snapped, pointing at Omar's knees.

"What's what?" Omar asked.

"What's that behind you?" Mom repeated. She motioned with her fingers. "Step aside, Omar. Let me see what you're hiding."

Omar slowly stepped aside. Mom looked down. Before she could say anything, Samkatt blurted out, "It's a snake habitat, Mrs. C-K. For Omar's snake." Samkatt always called Omar's parents Mr. and Mrs. C-K. It was easier to say than Choufik-Kassar.

Mom let out a shriek. "You don't have a snake in there, do you?"

"No, Mom," Omar said. "It's just the habitat where the

snake's going to live. Samkatt's neighbor Ray let me have it cheap. Five bucks."

"It's a real good deal," Samkatt added. Why couldn't he just shut up? Omar felt like kicking him.

"No comment," Mom said. She stepped into the hallway. Keeping her distance, she examined the habitat. "What's that curly stuff on the bottom?" she asked Omar.

"Just substrate, Mom. Bedding. Aspen shavings. It's organic," he hastened to add. "It covers the bottom of the habitat. Snakes like to crawl in it."

Mom raised her eyebrows. "They do, do they? There wouldn't be one crawling around in there now?"

"No, ma'am," Samkatt said. "There's nothing in there. Ray's snake died a long time ago. Do you want to take a look?" He pulled out the habitat lid.

"No!" Mom's voice jumped an octave. "Close it, Philip. Now!" she said. Samkatt shut the lid.

"Where are you taking it?" Mom asked Omar.

"To my room," Omar replied.

"No, you're not!" Mom said. "Who knows what kind of parasites are lurking in there! Take that habitat or whatever you call it outside. Dump all that bedding stuff in the recycling. Then take the habitat to the laundry room and rinse it with hot water. I mean hot! Then you wash it out with more hot water and a cup of bleach. Thoroughly! Use the scrub brush. Get into every corner and crack. Give it a final rinse with hot water. That should kill anything in it."

"If it doesn't kill us," Samkatt muttered. "A whole cup of bleach!"

"Bleach is cheap. Disease-carrying vermin are expensive," Mom snapped. "For now, just take the habitat outside. Then come back up to the studio. I have something to show you."

Omar and Samkatt hauled the habitat back downstairs. They carried it out the front door and set it in the driveway next to the garbage can.

"She wouldn't have come out of the studio if you hadn't thumped it down on the carpet. Couldn't you have been quieter?" Omar grumbled.

Samkatt shrugged. "And if she discovered it in your room? You know what kind of fit she would have thrown then? You should be grateful to me, man. I saved your butt."

"Yeah. Thanks a lot." Omar raced Samkatt back into the house and up the stairs. They found the studio door open. Omar's mom had a canvas on her easel. Omar and Samkatt couldn't see it when they first came in. She had it turned to the window to catch the light.

"Come around on this side so you can see what I'm doing," Omar's mom said. "I just began work this morning."

Omar had to blink twice to make sure his eyes weren't playing tricks. The rough outline of a painting filled the canvas, partly sketched with charcoal and partly filled with splashes and swirls of color. "Uh, is that what I think it is, Mom?" he asked.

Samkatt asked the same question. "I thought you didn't like snakes, Mrs. C-K."

"I don't. Not in the house," Omar's mom answered.

"That painting's in the house," Omar said.

His mom took up her brush and dabbed on a splotch of chrome yellow. "This is different. This is art."

Omar couldn't see the difference, although he didn't have any trouble seeing what his mom was creating on the canvas. It was most definitely a picture of a woman holding a snake. The snake was twining up the woman's arm so that it was facing her. Omar wondered why his mom would be freaked out by a real snake and then turn around to paint a picture of a woman holding one. A woman with full red lips, green eyes, and dark, curly hair—who, by the way, looked a lot like Mom.

"That's weird," Samkatt said. "What's it supposed to mean?"

"It's not supposed to mean anything," Omar's mom said. "I had a dream about snakes the night after Omar said he wanted one. It seemed like an interesting image. I thought I'd try painting it. I like it so far. How about you guys?" She splotched a dab of blue alongside the yellow.

"It's great, Mom! I love it," Omar said, not too convincingly. Another thought suddenly came to his mind. "You know, when I get my snake, I'll let you use it as a model."

Mom continued painting. "No thanks. I don't want to see your snake when you get it. I don't even want to know it's under the same roof as me, because the day I see it where it's not supposed to be is the day it's gone." She drove the point home with a slash of red.

"That's cold, Mrs. C-K," Samkatt said.

"That's our deal," Mom said. "Right, Omar? And you, Philip? When are you going to get serious about your art? Are you still drawing those ridiculous Japanese cats?"

"Yeah," Samkatt said. Omar felt him tense.

"You're wasting your time. And worse, you're throwing away your talent," Omar's mom said. "You should come over and sketch with me someday. I'll teach you how to really draw."

"Yeah, well, someday, maybe. We gotta go," Omar said, rescuing his friend. They hurried back downstairs. Omar noticed that Samkatt seemed unusually quiet. Mom must have really hurt his feelings.

"Hey, I'm sorry about my mom," Omar said as he walked Samkatt down the driveway. "She shouldn't have said that about your drawing."

"No problem, Omar. I'm cool with your mom," Samkatt said. "Maybe I ought to come by and let her teach me about drawing. Whoa! If I could learn to draw like her . . . I could go to Japan right now and get a job drawing anime!"

"All I want is a snake," Omar said.

"You have the habitat. Once you set it up, you're almost there. Catch you later, dude." Samkatt crossed the street. He waved goodbye as he and the wagon headed down the block.

* * *

Omar walked around to the two recycling bins beside the garage. Recycling was a big deal in Oregon. Newspaper, cans, and junk mail went into the blue bin. Yard debris, kitchen scraps, and anything that could be composted went into the green one. Omar raised the compost container lid. He took the water dish, the heat mat, the light, and the half-full sack of aspen shavings out of the habitat. Then he lifted the habitat to the edge of the compost bin and turned it over. The old bedding fell out. Omar brushed away a few strands of bark that had gotten caught on the lid. He blew into the habitat to scatter any remaining dust.

He was about to close the compost bin when he noticed something sticking out of the bedding he had just thrown away. It looked like a stick. A climbing stick? The online articles Omar had read about corn snakes were divided on whether or not they needed something to climb on. Some said yes. Some said no.

*May as well hold on to it,* Omar thought. He reached down to pluck the stick from the bedding. That was when he discovered it wasn't a stick.

It was a snake! A mummified corn snake, as dry and rigid as a twig. Omar let out a yelp. The snake slipped from his fingers. It dropped back into the compost bin.

Omar was more surprised than frightened. It took less than a minute for him to recover. He took a deep breath, then looked down into the green container.

The dead snake lay on the bedding. Faded colors lingered on its scales. Omar noted the red-and-white pattern. He remembered the pattern's name: "amelanistic." It must have been a pretty snake when it was alive.

How did it die? Knowing Ray, it wasn't hard to imagine.

The snake hadn't gotten enough heat. Or maybe Ray had let the habitat get too hot. Maybe he'd forgotten to feed the snake. Omar had heard somewhere that snakes can go without eating for a couple of weeks. A couple of weeks could easily stretch into a month. Had Ray remembered to change the water every day? Had he bothered to clean the habitat and change the bedding so the snake wouldn't get sick?

Or maybe Ray had just gotten bored and stopped doing anything. He might even have moved the habitat out to the garage and forgotten about it. The snake had crawled around in the cold and dark, looking for food and water. It must have tried to escape. Cold, thirsty, starving, it had burrowed into the substrate. Its life processes had slowed down until one day they'd stopped and the snake was dead.

Omar reached down. He gently picked up the snake again. He held it between his fingers as if it were a living creature.

"I'm sorry," Omar said. "You deserved better than that. You deserved a better owner than that loser Ray. You deserve better than this, to be dumped in the recycling."

Omar went into the garage. He got out his dad's spade. He dug a hole in the soft, rich earth of the rose bed. He placed the snake in the ground and covered it up. The snake would go back to the soil among the roses. It would become part of the rosebushes and their blossoms. When Omar's mom brought a bouquet of roses into the house, she would carry a part of Ray's snake with her. Red and white, just like the roses.

Omar made a vow as he stood by the snake's grave. "I won't be like Ray. I will take care of my snake. I'll do all I can to help it live and thrive. I will care for it as long as it lives. When it dies, I will give it back to the earth."

He stood in silence for several minutes, with his head bowed. Then he put the spade back in the garage and carried the habitat downstairs to the laundry room.

# chapter 5

"Omar! I'm going to pick up Zara now!"

Omar was still washing out the habitat when he heard Mom call from upstairs. It usually took an hour for her to drive to the day care center and get home. The drive itself took only fifteen minutes. But then she had to say hello to the other kids, parents, and teachers; gather up Zara's clothes, supplies, and art projects; say goodbye to the other kids, parents, and teachers; and then get Zara to the car and into her car seat. Nothing goes fast with little kids.

That worked out fine for Omar. He'd have the habitat sterilized, dried, and set up in his room by the time they got home. No remarks from Mom and no endless questions from Zara. *We're rolling!* he thought.

After putting on Mom's rubber gloves, Omar scrubbed the habitat, the lid, and the water dish with bleach and hot water. He scrubbed out everything there was to scrub. Then he turned the habitat upside down to drain in the laundry tub. Meanwhile, he ran upstairs to get a roll of paper towels from the kitchen and his mom's hair dryer from the bathroom. Yes, she'd have a fit if she knew what he was planning. But she wasn't going to know.

It took only about ten minutes to get the habitat and its equipment completely dry. Omar wiped the inside with paper towels and blasted it with the hair dryer until there wasn't a speck of moisture left. Then he put the hair dryer in the habitat and carried everything upstairs. He dropped the hair dryer off in the bathroom, making sure to put it back in the exact spot where he'd found it. Then he headed for his room.

He'd already cleared a place for the habitat on top of his dresser. It would get light from the window, but not direct sunlight, which could turn a glass enclosure like a snake habitat into a sauna.

Next, Omar opened the heat mat package. He turned the habitat upside down, peeled off the paper coating protecting the sticky side of the mat, and stuck the mat on the right third of the habitat's bottom. He made sure the cord was at the back corner so he could easily plug it into the power strip on the floor.

He placed an old towel on his dresser and put the habitat on the towel. The towel would keep the dresser's finish from being discolored by the heat mat. Omar had picked up that hint from an online reptile forum. He didn't need Mom blaming the snake for destroying her furniture. After that, he placed four old plastic furniture coasters from the kitchen junk drawer under the habitat's four corners. This was another hint he'd gotten online. Raising the habitat created space for air to circulate underneath, so the heat mat wouldn't overheat.

From then on everything was easy. Omar emptied the aspen shavings into the habitat and spread them around the bottom in a neat layer. Next, he filled the water dish with clean, fresh water and placed it at the opposite side of the habitat, away from the heat mat.

Omar added a cereal box with a hole cut in one side, along with an empty toilet paper tube. He put the box on the cooler side and the tube on the warmer side. The snake could hide and control its temperature at the same time. *I might add a climbing branch,* Omar thought. *Maybe later.* For now, he had the habitat completely set up. All that remained was to close the lid, set the heat lamp above the warm side, and plug it in.

He had just finished doing that when he heard the front door open, followed by feet charging up the stairs.

"Omar! OMAR!"

Zara was home. She burst into Omar's room. "Can I see the snake? Mommy told me about the snake."

"There is no snake," Omar said.

"What's that?" Zara pointed to the habitat on his dresser.

"That's where the snake is going to live. When I get it."

"Let me see!"

Omar lifted his sister under the arms so she could get a better view. "There's nothing to see, Zara."

Zara tapped on the side of the habitat. "There he is! I see him! I see the snake!"

"What snake? There is no snake."

"I see him!" Zara insisted.

Mom walked into the room. "What do you see, honey?" she asked Zara, taking her from Omar.

"Omar's snake. I see him. There! He's crawling in that stuff." Zara pointed to the aspen substrate.

"Oh, you're right! There he is! I can see him, too!" Mom said. Her eyes followed Zara's finger. "Isn't he beautiful!"

*Am I losing it?* Omar thought. *What's going on here?*

"What gives? I thought you couldn't stand snakes," Omar said to his mom.

"I can't. But there's no snake here," she said as Zara gleefully tapped on the glass.

"Then why are you pretending there is?"

"I want to encourage Zara to use her imagination," Mom said, as if that made perfect sense.

Maybe it did. But not to Omar. "Okay, but what if she wants to come in my room after I get the snake?"

"Let her," Mom said. "There's nothing wrong with Zara learning about snakes. They're interesting animals."

"I get it. Just not for you," Omar said.

"Just not for me," Mom agreed. She carried Zara out of the room. "We'll say goodbye to the snake, sweetie. He's going to take a nap, and you probably need a snack. Bye, snake!"

"Bye, Arrow!" Zara said.

"Who's Arrow?" asked Omar.

"The snake! That's his name, silly!" Zara said.

"How do you know that's his name?" said Omar.

"He told me," Zara said, as if that settled it.

"Arrow's as good a name as any," Mom said.

"Great!" Omar said after his mom shut the door. "I don't even have a snake yet, but I already have a name for him." He took his marking pens out of his desk drawer. He wrote "ARROW" on an index card in sky-blue letters and taped it to the side of the habitat. "Hello, Arrow," he said to the substrate. He had everything he needed, even a name.

It was time to get a snake. But where?

Omar wanted to discuss that problem with his dad after dinner. Omar had taken Dad to his room to see the habitat.

"Well done!" Dad said. "You bought this whole setup for five dollars? Excellent! You come from good merchant stock. Your Lebanese ancestors would be proud of you. So would the Pakistanis. May I make a suggestion? Your heat source should be plugged into a rheostat."

"What's that?" Omar said.

"It's a control for the heat mat," Dad said. "The heat mat plugs into the rheostat. You set the temperature you want. If the mat gets too hot, the rheostat turns it off. It protects your snake from getting cooked if the heat mat malfunctions. What kind of temperature does your snake need?"

"Seventy-five to eighty-five degrees is the usual range," Omar said. "It can get cooler at night."

"So we set it at eighty," Dad said. "You can raise or lower the temperature depending on whether the habitat's getting too hot or too cool."

"How can you tell?" Omar asked.

"I'll get you a couple of thermometers when I pick up the rheostat," his dad said. "You lay them down on the substrate. One for the warm end, one for the cool end. I've seen some that also measure humidity. The humidity level is something you ought to know if you're housing a reptile. The ones that live in the desert need low humidity. The ones that live in the jungle need high humidity. There's a lot more to taking care of a snake than throwing in a mouse every week."

His dad sure knew a lot about snakes. Omar was impressed. "Where did you learn all this?" he asked.

Dad sat down on Omar's desk. "I took a biology course when I was in college," he said. "I liked it. My professor got me a job working in the lab. I dissected dead animals and cared for live ones. Snakes included."

"Is that why you're not as freaked out about snakes as Mom?" said Omar.

Dad lifted his arms in a graceful shrug. "That's one reason. There's another."

"Okay, tell me," Omar said. He liked listening to his dad's stories about being a boy in Pakistan.

"Your mother is a city girl," Omar's dad began. "She was raised in a big house in Beirut with plenty of servants. She'd scream if she saw a cockroach. One summer when you were a baby, we took you to a park where there were grasshoppers. Your mother wanted to turn around and go home. I had to walk ahead and shoo the grasshoppers away before she would go on the path." Omar's dad started laughing.

"Now, me, I'm a country boy," Dad said. "Well, not one hundred percent. We lived in the city. But every summer my father sent me and my brothers to stay with our uncle in the country.

He wanted us to know our cousins and understand where our family came from."

"What did you do in the country?"

"We did what needed to be done. We planted. We weeded. We harvested. We herded animals. We drew water from a well. It was a fine experience. I wish you could do that. Maybe I could send you to spend a summer in Pakistan when you're older. It will certainly help you to understand how most of the world lives. No TV, no cell phones, no video games, no computers..." Omar's dad counted off the "nos" on his fingers.

Omar shuddered. Pakistan sounded like *Land of the Lost.* "What does that have to do with snakes?" he asked.

"I'm getting there," Dad said. "Now, I'm sure you know that where there is grain, there are rodents. Mice and rats. We can't blame them. They go where the food is. However, if you're a farmer breaking your back to provide for your family, you don't want hordes of rodents eating your crop. And I do mean hordes. One pair of mice can produce four to twelve offspring in twenty days. In less than a month, the babies themselves are ready to breed. Do the math."

"That's a lot of mice!" Omar said. He let it go at that.

Omar's father nodded. "Most villagers in Pakistan are afraid of snakes. They kill them on sight, whether or not they're dangerous. There are about a dozen kinds of poisonous snakes in Pakistan. Out of those, four can kill you. But most snakes are harmless, even helpful. A few centuries ago, the headman of my uncle's village figured out that if people left the snakes alone, they would pay the village back by eating the mice and rats that were devouring their crops. It worked. Since then, snakes have been popular in my uncle's village. My brother and I were taught never to harm a snake. The snakes even came into the houses. It isn't like America, where people start screaming if they see an animal in the house that isn't a dog or a cat. You'd hear a rustling at night, a squeak, then silence. You knew a snake had caught a mouse. Good! One mouse less means more food for us. That's why snakes were welcome everywhere in the village. Especially Daadi Samp."

"Who's Daadi Samp? Is that somebody's dad?" Omar asked. He'd never heard this story before.

"Oh, no! Definitely not!" Dad went on to explain. "Daadi Samp was a big black snake," he said. "'Daadi' in Urdu is what you call your father's mother: Grandma. 'Samp' means snake. So Daadi Samp means Grandma Snake. She was the biggest snake you ever saw. Certainly the biggest I ever saw. Every summer, after the harvest was in and the rats and mice started multiplying, my uncle and the rest of the village would go to the edge of the fields that bordered on a lake. They'd beat drums and bang gongs to summon Daadi Samp. And Daadi Samp, this huge snake, would come crawling out of the lake, through the fields, and into the village. Every house had a bowl of milk and a dish of butter set out for Daadi Samp, who was supposed to be over a thousand years old. I doubt that, although I wouldn't be surprised if descendants of the original Daadi Samp had been coming to the village for generations. When Daadi Samp showed up, the rats and mice fled. You could actually see them leaving town by the hundreds.

"Then one day the town gets a new mullah," Omar's dad continued. "Fresh out of the madrasah. This guy is determined to make changes. He hates snakes. He also hates the idea of people having anything to do with snakes. He keeps telling us they are wicked animals. Evil! Welcoming a snake to the village and offering her food was a kind of idol worship. Anyone who did that was going straight to hell.

"The people in town didn't take these warnings seriously. But one day the new mullah starts telling us he is going to get rid of Daadi Samp. He gets this big sword and walks around the village, saying he's going to cut Daadi Samp in pieces the next time she shows up. That's too much for my uncle and the other men. So one day, when the mullah is stalking around with his sword, the men come out and surround him. They gently take the sword away. They tell the mullah, 'Mullah, we love you. We respect you. You are a good man. But don't make us choose between Daadi Samp and you. You don't eat mice!'"

Omar's father burst out laughing. "'You don't eat mice!' That's what they said to the mullah. Isn't that a scream!" He laughed so hard that tears came out of his eyes. "'You don't eat mice!'"

Omar liked seeing his dad happy. However, the point of this story and why it was so funny escaped him. Maybe you had to grow up in Pakistan to understand it. It did have something to do with why his father liked snakes. Omar decided to build on that.

"I'm ready to get my snake. I just don't know where to get one," he said as his father wiped his eyes with his handkerchief.

Dad became serious again. "Good point. You should research that thoroughly. You want your snake to be in good health. You'll also need someone you can turn to if you have questions or need help. Have you tried the Web to see what's available in town?"

"Not yet," said Omar.

"Tell me what you find out," Dad said, standing up from the desk. It was time to get Zara ready for bed, which meant that Daddy had to read her a story.

"I will," Omar said. "And when I find out..."

His dad completed the sentence. "...we'll get your snake together."

# chapter 6

Omar started working on his assignment that evening before he started his homework. The first thing he did was Google "buying corn snake."

A lot of hits came up. Omar checked out the first five. They all said the same thing.

1. Get your snake from a responsible pet store or a reliable breeder. Look around when you go there. Are the habitats clean and well lit? Do the snakes have enough room and appropriate environments? Do you get a good feeling about the place and its staff?
2. Check the snake's habitat. Is the substrate clean? Is the water fresh?
3. A healthy snake will have clear eyes, a round body, and healthy skin free of bumps and sores. It should be active and alert, flicking out its tongue as it moves around its habitat.
4. Feeding is important. Ask when the snake last ate. There should be a record of when and what it

was fed. A young corn snake will eat every three or four days; an older snake, once a week. Ask if you can watch the snake being fed, even if that means coming back later. You want to make sure the snake has a good appetite. Some snakes are finicky eaters. Some won't eat at all. A snake that won't eat is not one you want. After watching the snake being fed—or better, feeding it yourself with guidance—you will know how to feed it when you get home.

5. Learn what the snake eats. Once a corn snake gets used to eating live mice, it may not accept frozen ones. Unless you plan to feed live mice to your snake, make sure it has been started on frozen mice.*** (Omar put stars after this point.)

6. Ask to hold the snake. It should feel muscular and strong. If it feels weak or limp, it may be sick. Turn the snake over and look at its belly. If you see dots that look like grains of black pepper, the snake has mites. Get your snake somewhere else.

7. Talk to the person who takes care of the snake you want to buy. Ask about feeding, shedding, and handling issues that you need to know about.

8. Locate a veterinarian in your area who specializes in reptiles. You will need to get medical help quickly if your snake becomes injured or sick.

9. Set up the habitat before bringing the snake home. Make sure the heat mat is functioning and that the warm and cool sides are at the correct temperatures. Provide several hides of different sizes at different parts of the habitat so that your snake can choose the one it prefers.

Take the snake home immediately and place it in the habitat.

10. Do not handle, feed, or bother your snake for a week after you bring it home. Allow it time to get used to its new surroundings.

*The habitat is set up,* Omar thought. *I just need the rheostat and the thermometers. Dad promised to get them for me. Now for the main event. Finding a snake.*

Omar Googled "corn snake pets wilsonville oregon." A long list of pet stores and corn snake breeders appeared on his screen. Just about every one, it seemed, in a hundred-mile radius. Omar checked out a few of the websites. They all seemed interesting and inviting. There was no way to really tell what a place was like without actually going there. Dad was willing to help out, but Omar couldn't ask him to drive all over the county. There had to be a way to narrow down the choices.

An idea popped into Omar's head. *There are websites that review films, DVDs, and music. Maybe there's one that reviews snakes.* He inserted a word into his Google: "reviews corn snake pets wilsonville oregon."

Another long list appeared. These consisted of chat room posts, business listings, and consumer reviews. Omar clicked on one. It turned out to be a really bad post about a pet shop in Canby. "Dirty...overcrowded...felt sorry for the poor animals..."

"Cross that one off my list," Omar said to himself. He clicked another. This was a little better, but hardly a rave. "This place mostly sells fish. Reptiles seem to be an afterthought. When I asked questions the owner told me he didn't know much about snakes. A high school kid comes in once a week to feed and take care of them."

Omar kept looking. He checked out dozens of posts in the chat rooms. A lot of them mentioned one store as THE place in the area. House of Snakes. The people writing the posts appeared to have been keeping corn snakes for years. Some were breeders themselves. If they all spoke so highly of House of Snakes, then that must be the place to go.

Omar opened another window and Googled "House of Snakes." He clicked on the first hit, www.snakehouse.com. Sure enough, a picture of a house appeared under the heading "House of Snakes." A tall guy with a beard stood on the lawn in front of the house. He was holding a snake in each hand. A notice at the bottom of the page said "Website Under Construction." It looked as if it had been under construction for a long time.

This did not look promising. Omar wondered if he had the right place. He had run into websites like this before. It was always the same story. Someone told a person that he ought to have a website for his hobby or business. So he tried designing and building one himself, only to abandon it when it got too hard or he got bored. Meanwhile, the half-finished website continued to float forever in cyberspace, a digital ghost ship forever doomed to sail the cyberseas.

Omar returned to the first window. He checked the House of Snakes posts. They were all fairly recent, within the past two months. Maybe House of Snakes wasn't defunct, though its website might be. He went back to the second window and took a harder look at the page.

Nothing! No business hours. No phone number or address. *Weird*, Omar thought. Then, without really thinking, he clicked on the picture.

Another page opened. This one was empty except for a button: "Contact Me." That was all.

Omar clicked on the button. An e-mail form appeared on the screen. Omar wrote in the message space:

Hello! I want to get a pet corn snake. This will be my first snake. I have been learning about corn snakes on the Internet. I have a habitat set up. Now I need a snake. I've seen a lot of posts that recommend House of Snakes as a good place to get a snake. I would like to come over with my dad to meet you and look at your snakes. When is a good time to do that? Please e-mail back.

He signed his e-mail "Omar." Wait. It wasn't a good idea to give a stranger his real name. Omar deleted "Omar" and wrote "Keeper of Snakes" in its place. That was what Dad had called him. It would do. Omar hit the Send button. He heard a whoosh as his e-mail whizzed off to some cyber-snakeland.

Omar waited. He hoped an answer might come whooshing back before he had to go to bed. Meanwhile, he started on his homework. The Big O must have been in a good mood. There were only twenty easy spelling words to practice, ten review math problems, and a grammar work sheet about commas. Omar left his computer on as he zipped through the assignments. He looked up every few minutes, hoping to hear that little bell indicating that e-mail had arrived.

It still hadn't rung by the time he was ready for bed. He brushed his teeth, said good night to his parents, tiptoed into Zara's room to give her a good-night kiss, and went to bed. He didn't stay up to read anything. He turned off the light and laid his head on the pillow.

Maybe—just maybe—he'd hear the bell before he shut his eyes.

"Omar!"

It was morning and his mother was calling for him to get up. In the bustle of Omar getting ready for school, Dad getting ready for work, and Mom getting Zara ready for day care, Omar didn't have time to check his e-mail. He was halfway to school with Samkatt when he remembered.

"I found this snake guy online. Everybody says he's the one to go to," Omar told Samkatt. Omar was lugging his backpack. Samkatt skated alongside on his board.

"What's his name?" Samkatt asked.

"Dunno," Omar said. "The website's name is House of Snakes."

"Sounds like a horror movie," Samkatt said. "Can't you just see it? Slime dripping down the walls. Blood oozing down the stairs. Skeletons on the floor. And snakes! Thousands of 'em! Snakes everywhere! Just like that scene in that movie *Raiders of the Lost Ark!*"

"Cut it out," Omar said. "I may have to go there. How am I going to get my snake if you keep creeping me out?"

"I have to draw this," Samkatt said. "Can't you just see it? *Omar's Excellent Snake Adventure!*"

"I don't want an adventure. I just want a snake," Omar told him.

Omar's excellent snake adventure began when he got home. He dropped his backpack, ran upstairs, and checked his e-mail. Sure enough, the number "3" covered the mail icon. Three messages waiting.

Two were spam: super saving discounts at Walmart and a woman in Nigeria offering to give him a hundred million dollars. The third was the one he was waiting for.

Yo, Keeper of Snakes!

You came to the right place. I'll be happy to meet with you this weekend if that's okay with you. We'll talk about snakes and I'll show you some you might like. The address is 2746 SE Hancock in Portland. Come by anytime Saturday between ten and four. The doorbell's busted, so knock real loud.

Looking forward to meeting ya! Any friend of snakes is a friend of mine.

SNAKE DUDE

"Awesome! He wrote back," Omar said to himself. He hit the Reply button and sent back his own e-mail.

Dear SNAKE DUDE,

Thanks for writing back to me. I think I can come out on Saturday. I have to talk to my dad. Maybe I will get a snake from you.

Looking forward to meeting you, too.

Keeper of Snakes

"I'm going to get a snake! I'm going to get a snake!" Omar sang to himself as he hit Send.

# chapter 7

"Hancock? Is that where it is?" Omar's mom said as she dished out the curried rice. "If you weren't going to look at snakes, I might go with you. Lots of interesting stores on Hancock. I used to exhibit my paintings in a gallery on Hancock when we first moved to Portland. There was this great coffeehouse—"

Mom didn't get to finish her story about the coffeehouse because Zara suddenly announced, "I don't like curry rice."

"No, no, no! You love curry rice," Dad said.

"Here we go again," said Mom. "Time to bring out the monkeys and the crocodile."

"I think that's getting old," said Dad.

"Can I say something?" Omar said.

"Go ahead," said Dad.

"Hey, Zara!" Omar began. He wiggled his fingers to get her attention. Zara stared across the table at him. "If you eat your rice, I'll let you play with my snake."

"What snake? You didn't get a snake, did you?" his mom asked.

"The invisible one," Omar whispered to her. "Remember?"

Omar's mom mouthed the words *Oh, I see.* She filled a spoon with rice. "Come, Zara, dear. Let's finish your rice and then we can all go see Omar's snake."

"His name is Arrow," Zara said. She gobbled her rice. "All gone!"

"Let's go see the snake."

Omar and Dad gathered up the dinner plates and stacked them in the sink. Then they all went to Omar's room. Zara rushed to the habitat.

"There's the snake! I see him!" she said, pointing into the empty glass tank.

Omar winked at his dad, who nodded back. "What color is the snake, Zara?" Omar asked his sister.

"Blue!" she said.

"A most unusual color," Dad said. "I don't believe a blue snake has ever been observed in the animal kingdom."

"Zara, would you like to hold the snake?" Mom asked.

Omar got the hint. "Sure, you can hold the snake, Zara," he said. "He won't bite. Hold out your hands. I'll get him for you."

Zara held out her hands, becoming so excited she could hardly stand still. "I want to hold the snake! I want to hold the snake!" she repeated.

"You have to stand still, dear," Dad said. "If you jump around too much, you'll frighten the snake. You don't want to do that, do you?"

"No," Zara said. She forced herself to stand completely still while Omar slid out the habitat's wire mesh lid. Reaching deep into the aspen shavings, he pretended to be catching the snake.

"No! Over here!" Zara yelled. She pointed to the opposite end of the habitat. "There he is!"

"Zara, don't shout," Mom said. "Snakes don't like loud noises. Neither do I."

Omar wondered how his mom knew that snakes didn't like loud noises, or why she cared, given how she felt about snakes. Or why it mattered, since there was no snake in the habitat anyway. He ran his hand through the aspen substrate.

"Am I getting closer?" he asked Zara.

"Yeah! Yeah! Oh...you almost have him!"

Omar gently closed his fingers around empty space. "Here he is!" he exclaimed. He lifted the invisible snake out of the habitat. "I'm going to put him in your hands now. Hold him firmly, but not too tight. Don't squeeze. Don't yell. Stand quietly and hold the snake gently."

Omar pretended to put the snake into Zara's hands. Zara tightened her right hand as if coiling her fingers around a snake's body. She placed her left hand above it, stroking the imaginary snake with her fingers.

"Am I doing it right?" she asked Omar.

"Yes. Perfectly," Omar said. Zara held up the snake so Mom could see.

"Look, Mommy! I'm holding the snake."

"Yes, I see," Mom said. "You're doing a very good job. He's a lovely snake."

"He's blue," Zara said. "His name's Arrow."

"I know," Omar said, pointing to the card he'd taped to the habitat. "Can you read that, Zara? I wrote his name for you. Can you read it? The letters say 'A-R-R-O-W.' That spells 'Arrow.'"

Zara stared at the letters on the card, stroking the snake at the same time. "Arrow. I can read. That says 'Arrow.'"

"Very good," said Mom. "I think it's time to put Arrow back in his cage."

"It's a habitat, Mom," Omar said.

"Okay. Hab-i-tat." Mom dragged out the word. "Come, Zara. All this excitement is making Arrow tired. It's time to put him back in his...hab-i-tat."

Dad lifted Zara up so she could reach down into the habitat. She set her fingertips gently on the bottom and waited for her imaginary blue snake to crawl off into the substrate.

"Goodbye, Arrow! See you tomorrow!" Zara waved through the glass after Dad set her down.

"He's waving goodbye to you, too," Omar said. "Can you see him? He's wiggling his tail."

Zara pressed her nose against the glass. "There he is! I see him!"

"I see him, too," Mom said. She began herding Zara toward the door. "Come, honey. It's time for your bath. Then we'll get ready for bed. First a story, then lights-out."

"Will you read me a story about Arrow?" Zara asked.

"I'll make up a story about Arrow just for you," Dad replied. He winked at Omar. "Good job, son!" he said as he accompanied Zara down the hallway toward the bathroom.

"Yes, that was excellent," Mom said. "I especially liked how you chose the name Zara wanted. You didn't have to do that. That was sweet of you."

"I know," Omar said. "You see, Mom, snakes aren't so bad."

"Not when they're invisible and don't exist," Mom said. "The real ones are altogether different." She patted Omar's cheek as she walked into the hallway. "Nice try. But you haven't convinced me."

*Not yet,* Omar thought.

# chapter 8

Omar looked at the house number he'd written down on a scrap of notepaper, then at the houses along Hancock Street. "It's that one," he told his dad. "The one with the fence. Third from the corner."

Omar's dad drove slowly along the street. "I'll drive. You keep your eyes open. Yell when you see a parking space."

"Do you think you'll find one?" Omar asked. "It looks pretty crowded." They were only a few blocks away from the weekend farmers' market. All the streets were lined with cars.

"Of course I'll find a space!" Dad said. "Don't I always? You have to have faith, Omar. You have to believe that the space exists. No faith, no space. Faith makes it happen."

"You sound like one of those TV preachers, Dad," Omar said.

"You have to believe, Omar. Believe!" Dad reached over and gripped Omar's forehead with his big hand. "Believe, my son. Believe!"

"Okay, okay! I believe!" Omar said, laughing.

"Good! Now look for a parking space. It's here."

Omar studied the houses as his father drove up and down one block after another. Omar liked coming to Portland. The neighborhoods looked so different from the cookie-cutter houses and manicured cul-de-sacs of the suburbs. Here, only the big streets had names. The others were numbered. The whole neighborhood was laid out in a precise grid. The rectangular blocks were all the same size. The streets intersected at ninety-degree angles. There were no wandering lanes or meandering trails leading to dead ends. Or muddy fields where a developer had run out of money.

The houses here had been built a long time ago. The first thing you noticed was that each one had a front porch. The first thing you noticed about the houses in Omar's neighborhood was the garages.

Omar guessed that the people who lived in these houses didn't have much money, or at least, not as much as the people who lived in his neighborhood. Thick carpets of green moss grew on most of the roofs. Some looked as if the moss were the only thing holding the roof together. He saw fences with big chunks missing, junglelike front yards, and beater cars, with only one or two wheels, raised up on cinder blocks in a couple of driveways and even on a couple of lawns. Some people would call a neighborhood like this run-down. Not Omar. If he had to pick a place to live, it would be here. Because of the houses.

They were painted crazy colors. Deep purple. Hot pink. Sky blue. Plus a rainbow of other hues whose names Omar could only guess at but that Mom would surely know: indigo, turquoise, vermilion. It wasn't as if each house were painted just one color. The painters had used all of them. The door might be red and the siding might be blue. Each step, each porch railing might be a different color. It was as if someone in the neighborhood had gotten hold of a truckload of different paint cans and set them in the middle of the street for the whole neighborhood to have a housepainting party.

Omar wished at least one person in his neighborhood had had the nerve to paint his house screaming violet, with a crimson door and daffodil-yellow windows, instead of sensible, muted forest and earth colors.

For a moment he thought about asking his dad if they could move here. That would be exciting. They could live in a three-story house. Omar could have the whole attic for himself and his snake. His mom could paint the house any way she liked. She could put faces and sunbursts and rainbows all over the walls, with a huge blue snake twining around the front door so that the house looked like one of her paintings.

Omar was decorating the house in his imagination when he noticed a van's taillights going on. "That van! It's pulling out!"

Dad slowed the car to a stop and waited. "Believe, believe...," he chanted.

"I believe ... I believe ...," Omar chanted with him.

Sure enough, the van pulled out, leaving behind a parking space big enough for a couple of cars. Dad whizzed right in. He and Omar shared a high five.

"Did I call it? Was I right?" Dad said.

"You're always right, Dad," said Omar. "You're the man!"

Omar and his dad walked two blocks to Number 2746. Together they headed up the rickety front steps. Omar knocked on the massive oak door. No answer. He remembered the e-mail: "The doorbell's busted, so knock real loud."

Omar made a fist. He pounded on the door.

*Bang! Bang! Bang!*

"Okay, I hear you. I'm coming."

The door opened. Omar looked up. And up!

A giant stood in the doorway. He looked big enough to be Paul Bunyan's twin brother. A full red beard came down to his chest, covering the bib of his overalls. This must be the kind of guy who had to wear overalls because he couldn't find pants that fit. *Or maybe they just don't make pants that big,* Omar thought. Under the overalls the man wore a red plaid flannel shirt, and beneath that, a long-sleeved chocolate-brown thermal knit undershirt. Omar wondered about that. Why was the guy wearing an undershirt? It wasn't cold enough for that many layers. A thick copper bangle circled the man's right wrist.

Despite the black bandanna printed with skulls that was tied around his head, the guy didn't seem scary. Just big. His wide blue eyes and a dusting of freckles across his nose made him look more like a kid than a grown-up. A kid with a silver skull-and-crossbones stud in his left ear.

He held out a hand the size of a shovel and said, "Yo! I'm the Snake Dude. You must be..."

"Keeper of Snakes," Omar said. "But Omar is my real name. My dad's here with me."

"What do you want me to call you?"

"Omar, I guess. Keeper of Snakes sounds kind of stiff."

"Good enough for me," the Snake Dude said. Omar realized he was still shaking the Snake Dude's hand. He looked down and let out a yelp. The copper bangle on the Snake Dude's wrist suddenly stuck out its tongue.

Omar jumped back a foot. "Eeeek!"

"It's a snake!" said Dad. He didn't seem as startled as Omar. That could be because he wasn't that close.

"Ooops! Sorry about that," the Snake Dude said. "I forgot I still had him on my wrist. Omar, meet Ernie. Ernie's a ball python. Balls make good starter snakes, though they can be more finicky about eating than corns. They're not as active as corns. Corns like to move around. Balls stay put. Want to hold him?"

"Sure!" said Omar.

"Great. Here's the first lesson. Sterilize your hands before and after handling a snake. You should do it with every animal." The Snake Dude dug in his overalls pocket for a bottle of hand sanitizer. Omar squirted a dollop into his hands and rubbed them together. He wondered if this might be some kind of test, to see if he was comfortable around snakes. He held out his right arm. The Snake Dude unwrapped Ernie and wound him onto Omar's wrist. The snake's body felt cool. It didn't squeeze. It held Omar's wrist just tightly enough to keep itself in place. *It feels like living metal,* Omar thought. He stroked the snake with his left hand. The snake's body tightened slightly, but it didn't move away.

"May I try?" Dad asked. He squirted some sanitizer on his hands.

"Sure!" the Snake Dude said. "By the way, I'm the Snake Dude, if you're okay with calling me that."

"That's fine. Dude, I'm Dad, if you're okay with that." They shook hands.

"Sure! Omar, why don't you let your dad hold Ernie? Just unwrap him slowly. Like that. Support his body. Slow and gentle. That's how you do it."

Omar unwound the snake from his wrist and placed it on his dad's arm. He held it steady as the snake coiled itself around Dad's wrist. "It's like having a living wristwatch!" the Snake Dude said.

"Better!" said Dad. "This watch eats mice."

The Snake Dude thought that was pretty funny. Omar rolled his eyes, remembering the story about the snake Daadi Samp back in Pakistan. He hoped Dad wouldn't start telling that one again.

"Well, what do you say we go inside and get down to business? I know you folks have other things to do today," the Snake Dude said. He reached out to take Ernie from Dad. That was when Omar realized that the Snake Dude wasn't wearing an undershirt at all. What looked like a sleeve was really a tattoo. And not just any tattoo. The Snake Dude's arms were tattooed in a pattern of snake scales just like Ernie's! Omar glanced up at the Snake Dude's neck. There was the same pattern. It must cover his whole body, except for his hands and his head.

The Snake Dude had given himself a snake skin! He had come as close as a human could to turning himself into a snake. AWESOME!

Omar and his dad followed the Snake Dude into the house. Omar glanced around the living room. He expected to see an eighteen-foot python curled up on the sofa. There was no python. There was no sofa. There was no coffee table or TV. There was hardly any living room to speak of. All four walls were lined from floor to ceiling with steel industrial shelving. Habitats of different shapes and sizes filled the shelves. Some were lit up. Some were dark. Some were decorated with wood, stone, and plastic foliage. Some held only a hide and a water dish. Omar bent down to look into one of the hides. A pair of eyes looked back.

*How cool is this?* Omar thought. *The Dude's turned his house into a snake habitat!* Yes, this was the place to come to.

The Snake Dude opened a habitat lid and put his hand inside. Ernie moved across the substrate. Within seconds, he had disappeared into the hide.

"Welcome to my house. Or maybe I should call it my habitat," the Snake Dude said as they all sterilized their hands again. "I'll show you anything you like. We can fool around with snakes all day. Except I know Omar's interested in corns. Maybe that's where we should start." He looked at Omar. "You really want a corn snake?"

"Yeah," Omar said.

"Why?"

Omar hadn't expected that question. He thought carefully before answering. "Because I've never taken care of a snake before. I think it would be interesting because I'm interested in snakes. I know I would learn a lot from the experience. I've done a lot of research online. Everything I've read says that corn snakes are good snakes for beginners. They have good appetites. They don't need special diets or special habitats. They're generally good-natured. They get used to being handled." He could have gone further, but a nod from the Snake Dude told him he'd given a good answer.

"If you get a snake from me today, where will you keep it?"

That was an odd question, Omar thought. "In its habitat. In my room," he said. Where else would he keep it?

"The habitat's all set up?"

"Yes," Omar said.

"Tell me about it."

"You mean describe it? Okay," Omar said. "It's a twenty-gallon-long reptile habitat. Glass walls. Locking screen lid on top."

"What are you using for substrate?"

"Aspen shavings," Omar said. "For now. I got a half package cheap. Should I continue with it?"

The Dude shrugged. "You can if you want to. Newspaper works just as well. It's not pretty, but the snakes don't care. Aspen's fine if you don't mind spending extra money. Got a water dish? Hide?"

"Yes," Omar answered.

"How about a veterinarian? You need somebody who specializes in reptiles."

"Not yet," Omar said.

"Can you recommend someone?" Dad asked.

The Dude nodded. "Dr. Duggan at the Clackamas Clinic in Oregon City. She's the best. All the serious breeders go to her. I'll e-mail you her phone number and address. You also have me. Give me a call if anything doesn't look right."

"Thanks!" said Omar.

"Heat source?"

"A heat mat. It sticks to the bottom of the habitat. I have a heat lamp, too. I don't know if I'll use it."

"You can, but you don't have to. With corn snakes, a heat mat is all you need. One thing to remember: no heat rocks. Don't ever use them. Never, never, never! They'll kill your snake!"

The subject of heat rocks got the Dude totally steamed. His face grew red as his voice rose. He looked as if someone had plugged in a heat rock under him. "Never use a heat rock, Omar! They've killed more snakes than anything except cars. Snakes curl around heat rocks and don't realize they're being cooked until it's too late. Then the idiots bring the snake to me, as if I'm some kind of miracle healer who can fix the damage. Dude, you killed your snake because you were too stupid to learn how to care for it properly!"

Omar flashed on an image of Samkatt's neighbor, Ray, being strangled by the Snake Dude. *Dude! You killed your snake!*

"No heat rocks," Omar said. "I read the articles online. I know better."

"And I've gotten him a rheostat to control the heat output. And some simple gauges to monitor the temperature and humidity," Dad said.

"How many did you get?" the Snake Dude asked.

"Two," Omar said. "One for the warm side. One for the cool side."

"Good man! You've done your homework, Omar. Give me five. You too, Dad. You both know as much about setting up a habitat as a beginner can know. I think I can trust you with one of my snakes. Shall we check out a few?"

"Sure!" Omar said.

The Snake Dude led them to a hallway off the living room. He opened a door. Omar saw a staircase leading to a dark basement. "This way, dudes," the Snake Dude said.

# chapter 9

Omar and his dad followed the Snake Dude down a rickety wooden staircase. The Dude flicked on the light. Omar found himself in a brightly lit basement that went the length of the house. Like the living room, it had storage shelves lined up along the walls. Some of the shelves held habitats similar to the ones in the living room. Most, however, held plastic boxes, the kind Mom used to store woolen sweaters over the summer so moths wouldn't eat them.

The Snake Dude held out his arm like a king welcoming guests to his palace. "This is the Snake Room. Here are the snakes. Take a look around. If you have questions about anything, just ask me."

"What kind of snakes are these?" Omar asked.

"Corn snakes. Down here is where I keep my breeding stock and hatchlings. Let's have a look." Omar and his dad followed the Snake Dude between the shelves, looking at the snakes in the habitats and boxes.

"Are you sure all of these snakes are corn snakes?" Omar asked.

"Yup. Down here in the cellar they're all corns."

"Why do they look so different?" Omar said.

"That's the beauty of corn snakes," the Snake Dude said. "Wild snakes always came in different colors. Over the years, breeders created more. The two main colors are black and red. We can breed out the black to produce a snake that has no black pigment in its scales. That kind of snake is called amelanistic. Or we can breed out the red. That kind is called anerythristic. Don't try to say it. I had to practice a year before I could do it. Besides that, you can also breed to make some colors stronger or mute others. That's why there are so many different kinds of corn snakes: motleys, snows, ghosts, lavenders, bloodreds. It goes on and on. New colors and patterns show up every year. But they're all the same snake."

"Like people," Dad said. "People have different colors and body types, but we're all human beings."

"That's good! I'll have to write it down so I'll remember it," the Snake Dude said.

Omar stopped in front of one of the larger habitats. It looked to be about a yard long. Inside he saw a snake with a red-and-white pattern of scales. The snake was curled almost double. That would make it between five and six feet long. That was bigger than Omar! Its body was as thick as Zara's arm. Omar stared at the snake. The snake raised its head and stared at Omar. It stuck out its tongue. Then it turned away, gliding over the newspaper substrate into a cardboard box that Omar guessed was its hide.

"That's a big one!" Omar said.

"Yup!" the Snake Dude said. "That's Jenny. One of my best breeders. She's six years old. Really a special snake. Isn't she a beauty?"

"I didn't know corn snakes got that big," said Omar.

"Jenny's on the large side," the Snake Dude said. "Figure with corns they'll average about four to five feet once they hit adulthood. Still want one?"

"Yeah," said Omar. "But I don't think my habitat's going to be big enough."

"It's big enough," the Snake Dude said. "You'll start out with a juvenile. Your habitat will be fine for a couple of years. When your snake gets to be twice as long as its habitat, that's the time to move up to a bigger size."

"It's like a couple living happily in an apartment moving to a house when they have kids," Dad said. Omar didn't have to guess too hard to figure out who he was talking about.

"Want to see Jenny up close?" the Snake Dude asked.

"Sure!" Omar said. They passed around the sterilizer bottle again.

"Can you catch anything from snakes?" Dad asked, rubbing his hands.

"You mean, are they infectious?" the Snake Dude answered. "Usually not. Snakes are more likely to catch something from you than you are from them. Rats and mice spread disease. By eating rodents and keeping down their numbers, snakes actually keep us healthy. And snakes are fairly clean animals," he went on. "It's the substrate that isn't. Not surprising, considering they poop and pee in it. We try to keep it clean, but it's never going to be sterile. Snakes crawl through the substrate and burrow in it, so they're naturally going to pick up microbes that you don't want to have as your guests at the dinner table. Get the idea?"

"I see," Dad said. "Remind me to pick up a bottle of hand sterilizer for your room, Omar."

*Sterilizer,* Omar thought, making a mental note. He'd figured he had everything down, but he was finding out that there was still a lot to learn. And remember.

"It's even more important if you have contact with several snakes," the Snake Dude continued. "Unsterilized hands can transfer diseases from a sick snake to a healthy one. You usually can't tell if a snake is sick until it's almost dead. I've seen whole collections wiped out that way. So again, always—ALWAYS—

sterilize or wash your hands before and after handling any snake."

"Got it!" Omar said.

The Snake Dude opened the habitat. He reached inside and lifted the cardboard box. Jenny lay coiled underneath. She didn't try to get away as the Snake Dude lifted her up. His right hand supported the snake's middle. His left guided her head around as she tried to move away. Omar watched the snake closely. She didn't appear frightened. She didn't look as if she wanted to escape. She seemed curious, eager to explore the world outside her habitat.

"Watch how I'm holding her," the Snake Dude told Omar. "Like I said before, corns are more active than ball pythons. Jenny's going to want to move. Let her. One hand supports her body. The other turns her head back when you think she's gone far enough. She won't try to escape, but you need to pay attention to what's going on. Your grip should be firm, but not tight. Don't be too loosey-goosey, either. Corn snakes can move really fast. You get distracted and boom! Your snake's gone. Good luck finding it! A corn snake is never gonna wrap around your arm or shoulder like Ernie. If they're not resting, they're hiding or on the move. So when you take your snake out of its habitat, you have to give it one hundred percent attention."

"Your turn," the Snake Dude said. He held his arm close to Omar's. The snake crossed over. Now Omar was holding her in the crook of his right arm. He turned her head with the nudge of a finger. That was all it took. Omar soon had Jenny moving wherever he wanted her to go. He held her with his right arm while he stroked her body with his left.

"How does she feel?" Dad asked.

"Cool…smooth…like a rubber hose with a steel cable inside!" Omar had to reach for the right words. Holding a snake was like nothing he'd ever experienced before. Ernie, the ball python, was a lump compared to this. He felt Jenny's firm, supple muscles moving as she glided through his fingers. At times she would stare at Omar for a few seconds, stick out her tongue, then continue her restless glide.

"She seems fairly calm," Dad said.

"She should be," the Snake Dude replied. "Some kinds of snakes never get used to being handled. Not corns. I wouldn't say you could just go out and pick up a wild one. But snakes raised in captivity, like Jenny, get used to people. When I pick her up and take her out of her habitat, it usually means something interesting is going to happen. She'll have something new to explore. She might even get fed. My snakes only get good touches."

Jenny began to glide more rapidly. Omar found that she was getting harder to hold. "I think you'd better take her back now."

The Snake Dude took the snake from Omar's hands. "How about you, Dad? Want to hold her?"

"No, thank you," Dad said. "I'll admire from a distance."

The Snake Dude slipped Jenny back into her habitat. She glided across the substrate and back into her hide. "What's next?" he asked.

"Sterilize your hands," Dad said.

"Secure the lid," said Omar.

The Snake Dude grinned. "A-plus for both of you."

"I don't know," said Omar. "There's an awful lot to learn and remember."

"That's true," the Snake Dude said. "The good news is that corn snakes are hardy and forgiving. Ninety-nine times out of a hundred, they'll do okay if we try our reasonable best."

"Uh, Snake Dude...," Omar's dad said.

The Snake Dude and Omar turned in time to see Jenny pushing aside the lid of her habitat. Her head curled over the edge, the rest of her body preparing to follow. The Snake Dude let out a yell. He quickly put Jenny back inside.

"See what I mean?" he said to Omar after locking down the lid with the combination lock. "Thanks, Dad. She would have been out and gone before I noticed. Serves me right for flapping my jaw when I should be taking care of business. Which proves my point. You can have thirty years' experience handling snakes and still mess up. If I can mess up, Omar, so can you. Now let's get you a snake."

# chapter 10

The Snake Dude kneeled on the basement floor. He pulled a large white plastic box from a bottom shelf. Omar squatted to see better. Dad looked over his shoulder as the Snake Dude undid the side catches and lifted the lid.

Inside the box Omar saw newspaper substrate, a water dish, and a hide made out of a Cheerios box. The Snake Dude lifted the hide. Underneath was a snake. This snake was not nearly as big as Jenny. It was coiled with its head resting on its body. It looked to be about eight inches long, about as thick as a felt-tip marker, and mostly bright orange, with red blotches outlined in black on its back.

"That's a handsome snake," Dad said.

"It's an Okeetee," the Snake Dude said.

"What does that mean?" Omar asked.

"Okeetee's a color variation that occurs in nature. They aren't specially bred. The first ones ever found came from a place in South Carolina called Okeetee." The Snake Dude lifted the snake from the box. The little snake glided up and down his arm just the way Jenny had. "This one's a male. He's a really nice snake. If you like him, I'll make you a good deal."

"How can you tell it's a male?" Omar asked. He almost said "boy," but caught himself. "Male" sounded more scientific.

"You can see the difference in mature snakes. A female has a more tapered tail than a male does. Determining a snake's gender gets a little complicated when they're young. It's nothing a beginner should try for himself. You could hurt the snake. I can walk you through it later if you're interested. For now, I think you and Snake should get acquainted. Don't you?" the Snake Dude said.

"What do you think, Omar?" Dad asked.

All the online articles Omar had read about choosing a snake came back to him. He did like this snake. Everything about him looked good so far. But Omar still had some things to check out before he made up his mind.

"May I hold him?" he asked the Snake Dude.

"Sure!" the Snake Dude said. He leaned close to Omar so the snake could cross between them. Omar watched the snake as he glided back and forth, up and down his arm. The snake seemed alert. His eyes were clear. Omar couldn't feel any bumps as the snake moved through his fingers. The snake was used to being held. He didn't try to bite. Nor did he appear to be bothered by having a stranger handle him.

Omar turned the snake over to examine his belly. He was looking for little dark spots that indicated mites. He didn't see any. Nor did he see wounds or sores. No missing scales. The snake's body was round and firm, an indication that he was being fed a healthy diet and was eating regularly.

"No mites," the Snake Dude said. Omar felt embarrassed, but the Snake Dude was quick to reassure him. "I don't blame you for checking. It shows you've done your homework. I stand behind my snakes. Any snake of mine will pass any inspection you want to give it."

Omar believed that was true. The Snake Dude loved his snakes the way some people love their children. Omar guided the snake back and forth between his arms. Dad leaned over and whispered in his ear.

"You don't have to pick the first one you see. We can look around a little more. We can even go someplace else. Take your time. You don't have to make up your mind now."

"I know, Dad," Omar said. "But I really like this snake. Everything about him goes with what I'm looking for. He's friendly. He's healthy and well fed. He likes to be held. I don't really care about the color, although this one sure is pretty. He's not blue, like Zara's imaginary snake. But I don't think I'm going to find a blue one."

"If you do, let me know right away," the Snake Dude said. "Corns come in a lot of wild colors. As far as I know, blue isn't one of them. Not yet."

"Well? Are you ready to decide?" Dad asked.

"I have a couple of questions first." Omar turned to the Snake Dude. "This isn't a hatchling. Am I right? He's bigger, so he must be older. Is there something about him I should know?"

"I guess," the Snake Dude said, "I'll tell you what I know. That snake's a rescue. He's not one that I bred. A friend of a buddy of mine decided he wanted a snake, so he went out and got one. The problem was, he didn't check it out with his girlfriend. Wouldn't you know, turns out she's terrified of snakes. Couldn't stand to be in the same room with one. Not even under the same roof. The snake gave her nightmares. She had a real phobia. Of course, the dude thought he could get her over it, and sometimes you can. But not in this case. He had to choose: the girlfriend or the snake. The girlfriend had a job at a restaurant downtown and could cook really good, so the snake had to go."

Omar heard his dad laughing. He turned around. "Just like the mullah!" Dad said. "'You don't catch mice!' 'You can't cook!'"

"What's that?" the Snake Dude asked.

"Nothing. Just a private joke," Dad said. But Omar wasn't in a joking mood. He suddenly had something important to think about.

"Uh, Snake Dude. My mom doesn't like snakes, either."

The Snake Dude's face grew serious. "I hope you discussed

this with her, Omar. Some people are terrified of snakes. It's not fair to spring a snake on them. It's not fair to the person; it's not fair to the snake."

"I agree," Dad said. "Our family has talked about this. My wife has agreed to tolerate the snake as long as it stays in Omar's room."

The Snake Dude looked doubtful. "Well, Dad…Omar… I hate to say this, but I've heard that one before. Sometimes it works out. Sometimes it doesn't. Promise me this. If I sell you a snake and it doesn't work out, if having a snake in the house really upsets your mom, you'll bring the snake back to me. You won't let it go or give it away. You won't move it into the garage or basement to let it die. Call me anytime. I'll take it back. No questions asked. I mean that, Omar. I want your first experience with a snake to be a good one. I also want it to be a good one for your whole family." He held out his hand. "Promise?"

Omar shifted the snake to his left arm. He held it coiled around his left wrist while he shook the Snake Dude's hand with his right.

"That's fair and generous of you," Dad said.

"Like I said before, I'm not in it for the money. I do this because I love snakes and I want other people to learn to love them, too. They've gotten a bad rap over the years. Okay, folks! Enough philosophy!" The Snake Dude clapped his hands. "We're getting close to decision time. Do you like this snake, or do you want to see some others?"

"It's up to you, Omar," said Dad.

"I just have a couple more questions," said Omar.

"Fire away," said the Snake Dude.

"What's the snake's name? Does it have a name?" Omar asked.

"Yeah, my buddy gave the snake a name. But it's dumb," the Snake Dude said. "Alger. Alger Hiss. Get it?"

"No," said Omar. Dad snickered a little.

"Then never mind," said the Snake Dude. "Snakes aren't

dogs. They don't know their names. They don't come when you call them, so you can name him anything you like when you get home."

That satisfied Omar. He felt relieved not to have to explain to Zara that Arrow wasn't going to be the snake's name. Next question.

"When did the snake last eat?"

"I can tell you exactly," the Snake Dude said. An index card with the snake's feeding schedule—when he had last eaten and what he had eaten—was taped to the top of his box. "It's a good idea to keep a written feeding record. This snake last ate three days ago. Two pinkies. He'll probably be ready to move on to one fuzzy after he completes his next shed."

"What does all that mean?" Dad whispered to Omar. "Do you understand it?"

"Yeah, Dad. I'll explain later," Omar said. He turned back to the Snake Dude. "Can I see him eat?"

"Sure!" the Snake Dude said. "If you don't mind coming back."

"What do you mean?" Omar asked.

"A young snake usually needs five days to a week to digest its meal," the Snake Dude explained. "I'll wait a couple of days more before him I feed him again. If I give him a mouse now, he might not eat it. Even if he did, he'd still need another week before I'd let you take him home. Moving to a new habitat is traumatic for a snake. It's best to do it three or four days after a feeding. You'll also want to give him a few days more to get used to his surroundings before feeding him again. So if you want to see him eat, come back next week. We'll wait another week, and then you can take him home."

"I don't think I can wait that long," said Omar.

"You don't have to," the Snake Dude said. "Trust me. He's a good eater. You won't have any problems. Put him in his habitat when you get him home and leave him alone for the next five days. Don't handle him, don't bother him. Change his water.

Clean up any messes he makes. But that's it. He'll be fine once he settles in. By then, he'll be really hungry. He'll grab anything you offer him. That will get him used to taking his food from you. After that, you're over the hard part. Enjoy your snake."

"And what will we feed him?" Dad asked.

"Frozen mice," the Snake Dude said. "Plenty of snake keepers disagree with me, but I don't believe in feeding live mice to snakes. It's cruel to the mice and dangerous for the snake. A terrified animal will fight for its life. Mice have teeth and claws. They can do serious damage. A cut gets infected, and then you're looking at real trouble. Also, if the snake isn't hungry and doesn't eat the mouse right away, the mouse may start nibbling on the snake. Do you know where to get feeder mice, Omar?"

"Not really," Omar said. "I haven't checked it out yet."

"I'll give you ten to start you off," the Snake Dude said. "I buy frozen mice in bulk. A lot of snake keepers get their mice from me. You can, too, if you like. Or you may find someplace that's cheaper and closer. It's up to you. Ten should last for about two and a half months. That'll give you time to ask around and decide."

"Thanks, Snake Dude. I'll let you know," Omar said.

"Good. So now, if I've answered all your questions, it's time to cut to the chase. Do you want this snake, Omar?"

"Yes!" Omar said, beaming, as the snake glided up and down his arm. They both seemed as comfortable and relaxed with each other as if Omar had been keeping pet snakes for years.

"I think you made a good choice," said the Snake Dude. "I believe you and Alger will be happy with each other."

"So do I," Dad said.

"Arrow! That's his name now," said Omar.

The snake glided across Omar's shoulders and flicked out his tongue, as if to say he agreed.

# chapter 11

The drive home seemed endless. "Can't you go any faster?" Omar asked.

"The speed limit is sixty-five, Omar," Dad said. "I'm doing sixty-five. See for yourself." He pointed to the speedometer.

"Nobody does sixty-five, Dad!" said Omar. "Look out the window. Everybody's passing us."

Omar usually didn't care if his dad poked along. His dad always poked along when he got behind the wheel of a car. Omar's mom was the one who liked to drive fast. However, this drive home was different. The kitchen trash bag on Omar's lap held two precious cargoes. Omar had to get them home and where they needed to be as soon as possible.

Inside the bag were two plastic boxes. One held Alger Hiss, the snake, whose name was going to become Arrow as soon as they got home. The other, wrapped in a triple layer of newspaper secured with duct tape, held ten tiny frozen infant mice. Pinkies, these were called, because their newborn skin was pink. They were too young to have grown any hair.

Omar had been surprised to see how tiny pinkies were when the Snake Dude took them out of his freezer and showed them to him for the first time. A pinkie mouse was only as big as the end of Omar's little finger. Even so, that was enough of a meal for a small snake. In fact, a pinkie mouse was more like twelve meals. One pinkie could last a young snake three or four days. Snakes were amazingly efficient when it came to using food and energy.

Much more than people. That was the problem now. Omar had ten frozen pinkies in a Tupperware container. He had to get them home and into the freezer before they thawed. If the pinkies thawed too much, they might spoil. And Dad was going so slowly!

At last! The car turned off at the Wilsonville exit. Turn left, go under the freeway, follow the road past the fields, then another left into the development. Through the winding streets. Endless winding streets with a stop sign on every corner. Omar felt ready to scream. His dad insisted on coming to a full stop at every stop sign, even when there were no cars or people in sight. He cruised slowly down the streets, watching for kids on bicycles when there was not a kid or a bicycle to be seen.

"Mom would have gotten us home in half the time!" Omar said.

"Your mom would not be in a car with a snake," said Dad. Omar had to admit he was right.

Dad turned into their cul-de-sac. Omar pressed the button on the garage door opener. The door went up before the car reached the driveway. Dad parked the car in the garage. Omar unbuckled his seat belt. He was out the door before his dad turned off the motor. He ran to the freezer in the corner of the garage. Mom liked having a freezer so she could take advantage of grocery sales. She kept it stuffed. With luck, she would never notice one additional package.

Omar lifted the freezer lid. He buried the duct-taped box with the pinkies in it beneath chicken nuggets and frozen broccoli. Then he charged up the stairs and into the kitchen, clutching the box with Arrow inside.

"Are you back?" Omar heard Mom calling from upstairs.

"Yeah!" Omar yelled. "We got a snake."

"Fantastic!" Mom said, meaning the opposite. "I'm in the studio with Zara and I'm locking the door. You put your new friend in your room where it needs to be. Tell me when you've got it locked down. Then I'll come out. Not before."

Omar heard his sister yelling. "I want to see the snake! I want to see the SNAKE! *I WANT TO SEE THE SNAKE!*"

"I'm sending Zara out," Mom said. "Understand—once she goes out, she's not coming back in again until I know that snake is in its cage."

"Habitat, Mom!" Omar corrected her.

"Whatever!"

Zara came running down from upstairs. Dad came in from the garage. Omar waited for them in the kitchen.

"I want to see the snake!" Zara shouted, jumping up and down with excitement.

"Come upstairs with me," Omar said. "I have to put the snake in his new house. You can help me."

Zara raced upstairs to Omar's room. Omar followed. He held the plastic box carefully in both hands, trying his best not to shake it too much as he climbed the stairs. He imagined how upsetting all this commotion must be to Arrow. Especially Zara's screaming. Best to get him into his habitat and leave him alone in peace and quiet. *That's what I would want,* Omar thought as he pushed open his bedroom door with his shoulder. *Maybe snakes and people aren't all that different after all.*

Zara was already inside, bouncing on Omar's bed. "We have a snake! We have a snake!" she sang.

Dad raised a finger to his lips. "Shhh, Zara! Don't make so much noise. The snake is being introduced to his new home. We don't want to frighten him."

"I'll be quiet!" Zara said in what was hardly her quiet voice. Dad sat beside her on the bed to settle her down. "Go ahead, Omar," he said.

"We have to clean our hands first." Omar passed the bottle of hand sterilizer to Dad, who helped Zara with her hands, then sterilized his own. He passed the bottle to Omar, who did the same.

Zara sat quietly, wriggling with excitement but not making a sound. "Good job, Zara," Omar said.

"How are the readings?" Dad asked.

Omar glanced at the two thermometers and at the hygrometer, which measured humidity. "Eighty-nine degrees on the warm side; seventy-eight on the cool side," he said. "Fifty percent humidity. The water's fresh. I changed it this morning. Hides are in place. All systems go!"

"Looks good. Let's do it," Dad said.

"Snake...snake...," Zara keep saying. "I want to see the snake."

Omar opened the combination lock holding down the habitat's lid. He slid out the lid, then loosened the top of the Tupperware container. He set the box in the habitat on top of the substrate, midway between the hot and cool sides. "The snake can choose which way he wants to go," Omar whispered. He closed the lid and locked it. Then he pulled over his desk chair and sat down to watch and wait with Zara and his dad.

The lid moved. Zara jumped.

"Shhh! He's coming out. Don't scare him."

Zara held tight to Omar as the lid slipped aside. A blunt nose appeared. A small tongue flicked in and out, tasting the air. Then a head emerged.

Zara shook with excitement, but true to her promise, she didn't make any noise. Omar, Zara, and their dad watched as the snake glided out of the plastic box. Smoothly, silently, the snake appeared to float over the aspen substrate. He glided back and forth, from one side of the habitat to the other. He stopped by the water dish. Omar saw the water's surface vibrate.

"He's drinking!" Zara said in a loud whisper.

"That's a good sign," said Dad.

The snake glided back and forth a few more times. He stopped by one of the toilet paper tubes Omar had placed in the habitat as hides. He poked his head inside. The rest of his body followed. Soon only the tip of his tail could be seen, extending outside the tube.

"What's he doing?" Zara asked.

"He's resting," Omar said. "You'd be tired, too. He's had an exciting day, moving to a new house. Now he's going to take a nap."

"Can we see him when he wakes up?" Zara said.

"We're not supposed to disturb him," Omar said. "Let's let him sleep until he decides to wake up. Don't worry. If I see him moving around, I'll come and get you."

"Maybe he wants a snack?" Zara said.

"I don't think so," said Omar. "Snakes aren't like people. They don't eat every day. The Snake Dude told us he probably wouldn't be hungry for a while."

"Okay," Zara said. Omar was surprised that she accepted that fact so easily. Zara got up off the bed. She tiptoed to the habitat.

"Good night, Arrow. Sleep tight," she whispered. Then she bent down and kissed the glass, just across from the tip of the snake's tail. The tail wiggled and disappeared into the hide.

"Did you see that?" Zara said. "Arrow said good night to me. Snakes talk with their tails."

"I know," Omar said. Zara tiptoed across the room. She stopped by the door to wave goodbye.

"Good night, Arrow!" she said again. Then she was off down the hall.

"Looks like his name is going to be Arrow," Dad said.

"I like it better than Alger," Omar said.

"Arrow's a good name," Dad said. "Well, Omar? You're the snake expert. How do you think it went?"

"Pretty good," Omar replied. He knew he was far from

an expert. Still, bringing the snake home had gone according to plan.

The snake's choosing a hide in the middle of the habitat was a good sign, too. It meant that the temperature inside was just about right. Omar could see the advantage of using toilet paper tubes and cardboard cereal boxes as hides. They were light enough for Arrow to move around if he chose to rearrange his furniture. So far, everything was A-OK.

Omar turned off the bedroom light and stepped out into the hallway, closing the door behind him. "What about food?" his dad said. "Do you have everything you need? We still have a few days before Arrow's first feeding."

"Can you get me a forceps, Dad?" Omar asked. "I should have some kind of long tweezers or tongs to hold the mice. You're supposed to keep your fingers out of the way. Snakes don't have good eyesight. They might bite you by mistake."

"I'll get you a pair of forceps," Omar's dad said. "I hope you realize that's not your real problem."

"I know," Omar said. His problem wasn't in the habitat. It was in the freezer in the garage. Because if there was one creature his mom hated more than snakes, it was mice. Keeping frozen mice in the freezer—even pinkies—was not an option.

But what other options where there? Omar needed to figure that out.

Fast.

# chapter 12

"I got a snake," Omar whispered to Samkatt on Monday morning. The Big O was giving the class its Monday dose of the weekly news. She had her laptop rigged to the SMART Board at the front of the room. She kept zapping the screen with blasts from her laser pointer as she zapped the class with bursts of information.

PIRATES ATTACK OFF MINDANAO...WHITE HOUSE PARROT...OIL INDUSTRY BAILOUT...

Omar found the pirates interesting. He didn't know where Mindanao was or anything about the oil industry. As for the parrot, Omar had never cared that much about birds. Now, if the president of Brazil had presented the White House with an anaconda...

Samkatt looked up from his sketching. His idea of taking notes was drawing pictures. Omar could see him working on a sketch of American soldiers shooting pirates full of bullets. The balloons above the pirates' heads said, "Yo-ho-ho!" The American soldiers were saying, "Hooray for America! Die, you pirate scum!"

Samkatt seemed lost in his drawing. He didn't appear to have heard Omar whispering. But the Big O had.

"Omar, the island of Mindanao belongs to what country?" The question came at Omar like a projectile fired from a rocket launcher.

"Uh...uh...," Omar stammered. He noticed Samkatt's pencil dancing across the page, writing a word. "Philippines."

"Philippines, Ms. Ortiz?"

"Is that an answer or a question? How do you feel about bailing out the oil industry?"

Omar could answer this one himself. "If it helps the country, it's a good idea. It's too early to tell. We'll have to wait and see."

He'd heard his dad say that many times. It was a good all-purpose comment you could make about anything in the news. Omar glanced over at Samkatt's desk and saw the words "NO!!!!!" and "Bunch of Crooks!!!" beneath "Philippines." Samkatt had even drawn a little sketch of men in striped prison suits breaking rocks with sledgehammers while other men beat them with whips. Samkatt obviously did not think bailing out the oil industry was a good idea. However, Omar didn't want to argue the issue with the Big O, especially since he didn't know anything about it.

"Sit down!" Ms. Ortiz snapped. Omar sat down, glad to be out of the line of fire. Once the Big O's attention returned to the SMART Board, he turned to Samkatt. "Thanks," he whispered.

"Don't mention it," Samkatt whispered back as he returned to his drawing. "You're wrong about bailing out the oil industry. It's a huge rip-off. My dad says so."

Omar didn't argue the point. He didn't care. He had something more important to share with Samkatt.

"You didn't hear me. I was trying to tell you. I got a snake."

"Cool!" Samkatt said. "When can I see him?"

"Not yet," Omar said. Arrow hadn't showed himself since

Omar had put him in the habitat. He was moving around, though. All the hides in the habitat had been rearranged. Arrow probably did that at night while Omar was asleep. Not surprising. Corn snakes were nocturnal animals. For now, it was just a matter of being patient and waiting until Arrow felt ready to come out.

Which he would most likely do when he got hungry.

"There's nothing to see," Omar continued. "He went in his hide and hasn't come out since Saturday. The Snake Dude we got him from said to leave him alone for about a week to let him get used to his habitat. Just being in a new place is stressing him out already. I don't want to stress him any more. He'll come out when he's hungry. Then I'll feed him."

"What do you feed him?" Samkatt asked.

"Little baby mice. They're called pinkies because they don't have any hair yet," Omar said. "They kind of look like chewing gum. They're about the same size, too."

"You've got little baby mice running around your house? How'd you talk your mom into that?"

"She doesn't know," Omar said. "They're not running around. They're dead. Frozen. The Snake Dude gave me ten. They're in the freezer in the garage. At the bottom."

"Oh, your mom will love that! Wait till she goes digging for Zara's chicken nuggets!"

"I know. I need to find another place. I'm working on it. Do you want to come to my house when I'm ready to feed Arrow?"

"Who's Arrow? Is that the snake?" Samkatt asked. Pirates forgotten, his pencil now sketched an enormous cobralike snake swallowing an equally gigantic rodent.

"Yeah," Omar said. "Zara liked that name. The Snake Dude got him from a guy who called him Alger."

Samkatt chuckled. "Alger? Alger Hiss! Whittaker Chambers. Joe McCarthy. Truman administration. That's funny!"

"How do you know this stuff?" Omar asked. "You must read a ton of books."

Samkatt shrugged. "I never read books. Reading takes too long. I watch The History Channel. Everything you need to know is on TV. Whatever isn't, is online." He put the finishing touches on the rodent. And they really were the finishing touches—Samkatt drew the rodent's hind end disappearing down the snake's gullet.

"Philip! What kind of parrot did the president of Brazil present to the American people?" The Big O's voice shot across the room.

"Scarlet macaw, Ms. Ortiz," Samkatt droned, as if it were as dumb a question as "When was the War of 1812?" and "Who's buried in Grant's Tomb?" He went on with his drawing.

*I wonder why she bothers?* Omar thought. Samkatt was the kind of kid who didn't really need to go to school. And sometimes it truly did seem that anything anyone needed to know was on TV. Omar wondered if his parents were wrong. Maybe they should let him watch more TV so he could be as smart as Samkatt. Omar didn't waste much time on that thought. He knew how far it would get in his house. About as far as asking his mom if he could keep frozen mice in the freezer. Which brought him back to the main question.

What was he going to do about those mice?

Omar still hadn't come up with an answer by the time the dismissal bell rang. He plodded home, bent beneath his backpack. Samkatt skated alongside on his board.

"Let's go over to your house," Samkatt said. "I want to see your snake."

"There's nothing to see," Omar said for what must have been the twelfth time that day. "He's in his hide. He won't come out and we're not supposed to disturb him."

"I won't disturb him," Samkatt insisted. "He can stay in his hide. I don't want to touch him. I just want to see him."

"But there's nothing to see!" Omar said again.

"I'll see whatever there is to see," Samkatt replied.

The argument went back and forth until they reached Omar's house. "Since we're already here, I may as well go up and have a look," Samkatt said with a definite note of triumph in his voice.

Omar didn't bother to argue. He found the door unlocked. He wiped his feet carefully on the mat before going in. Samkatt did the same. They both knew from bitter experience how Omar's mom felt about mud and dirt being tracked across her living room. Samkatt parked his skateboard in the hall closet with his coat. He knew that Omar's mom was even less fond of greasy skateboard wheels.

"Mom, I'm home! Samkatt's with me!" Omar hollered upstairs.

"Hey, Omar! Hi, Philip!" Mom called down. "I'm finishing up in the studio. Then I'm going shopping. It'll probably take me an hour or so. I have to pick up Zara at day care after that, so I'll be gone until about five. Are you boys hungry? There are snacks in the fridge."

"We're cool, Mom," Omar said.

"Yeah, Mrs. C-K," Samkatt said. "I came to see Omar's snake."

"Wonderful!" Mom said. "Give Snakey my regards."

"Mom! His name's Arrow. You know that!" Why did she have to be so sarcastic all the time? It was getting annoying. Omar was about to say something when Samkatt nudged him with his elbow.

"Ancient Chinese proverb: Never tee off Mom when you keep mice in freezer."

"You're right," Omar said. "Let's go to my room."

"This is awesome!" Samkatt said as they started walking upstairs. "We have the whole house to ourselves. You, me, and Alger."

"Arrow," Omar corrected him. He paused when he reached his bedroom. "We don't want to scare him if he's moving around. Don't make any noise or sudden moves. Don't tap on the habitat, either."

Samkatt nodded to show he accepted the rules. Omar opened the door slowly. He could see across the room to the habitat on the dresser. Something was moving.

Arrow! The snake had come out of his hide. Omar watched him gliding back and forth across the substrate, from one end of the habitat to the other, flicking out his tongue, tasting the air. Omar turned to Samkatt. Pressing his finger against his lips, he beckoned to Samkatt to follow him into the bedroom. Samkatt tiptoed in behind Omar. Neither boy made a sound. They sat down on the edge of the bed so quietly that not a spring squeaked. If the habitat had been a stage, the bed would have been front-row seating.

"He's looking for something," Samkatt whispered.

"I think he's hungry," said Omar.

"When did you last feed him?"

"I didn't. The Snake Dude fed him three days before I brought him home."

"Three days!" Samkatt said. His voice caught Arrow's attention. The snake stopped, staring in their direction. Omar and Samkatt froze. Arrow waited, then moved on. Samkatt leaned over to Omar and whispered in his ear, "It's been three days since you brought him home. That means he hasn't eaten in close to a week? I'd be dead if nobody fed me for a week."

"Snakes are different. They can go a long time without food," Omar said.

"'Can' doesn't mean 'should,'" Samkatt said. "He's your pet, dude. If your snake's hungry, you gotta feed him. What's the problem?"

"I'm not sure how to do it. I never fed a snake before," Omar said.

"How hard could it be?" Samkatt said. "Toss in one of those baby mice."

"It's not as easy as that," Omar said.

"It won't get easier if you just sit around," Samkatt said. "Look, Omar. Your mom's not here. Neither is Zara. This is a perfect time to feed your snake and for you to learn how to do it. There's nobody around to bother you or get in your way or tell you how gross the whole business is. Your snake is hungry, and I want to see how he eats a mouse. Let's do it. What's stopping you?"

Omar knew exactly what was stopping him. He wasn't sure he could handle feeding a mouse to a snake. Even a frozen dead mouse. He'd read about how to do it in books. He had seen videos of it being done on YouTube. But to actually do it himself?

"I'm not sure I know how," Omar said. Then he told Samkatt the truth. "I'm not sure I can."

"Well, I can," Samkatt said. "Show me the mice."

# chapter 13

Omar and Samkatt headed back downstairs to the garage. Omar lifted the freezer lid. He dug around beneath loaves of whole wheat bread, toaster waffles, chicken nuggets, hamburger patties, an assortment of vegetables, and cartons of ice cream, all frozen hard as cannonballs, until he found what he was looking for. A square package wrapped in newspaper and duct tape. The cold air inside the freezer had cause the duct tape to lose its stickiness. It had already begun to pull away from the newspaper. Omar completed the job. He pulled off the gummy mess of tape and paper and tossed it into the garbage bin.

"Is that it?" Samkatt said, pointing to the plastic container in Omar's hands.

"Yeah," Omar said. He shook the container. The frozen pinkies inside rattled like marbles against the plastic.

"Let's see them," Samkatt said. He leaned over for a closer look as Omar pried the lid off the container. The frozen baby mice did look like chewing gum. Or pink pencil erasers. "Can I touch them?" Samkatt asked.

"Go ahead, if you really want to," said Omar. He handed the

container to Samkatt, who was a lot more eager to touch the mice than he was.

"They're frozen solid," Samkatt said, rolling one of the pinkies around in his fingers. "They're kind of like frozen peas, except they're pink instead of green. What do you do with them? Do you feed them to the snake like this?"

"No," Omar said. "We have to thaw them out first so Arrow will think they're alive."

Samkatt started laughing. "Dude, if that snake thinks these little guys are alive, he's either blind or stupid!"

Omar wasn't in the mood for jokes. If Arrow refused the pinkies, then Omar had a really big problem. "It doesn't matter what he thinks. It matters that he recognizes them as food and eats them."

"Okay, what do we do?" Samkatt said.

"Pick two pinkies. The Snake Dude says Arrow usually takes two, since he's bigger than a hatchling."

Samkatt poked around in the freezer container. "Eeny, meeny, miney, mo...you're the mouse who gets to...GO!" He picked out two pinkies that way. He placed them in the palm of his hand. "How about these guys?" he said, showing them to Omar.

"Yummy!" Omar said. He put the lid back on the freezer container and shoved it back into the freezer, as deep as he could. He closed the freezer lid and headed for the kitchen. Samkatt followed, clutching the pinkies.

"Hurry up! They're melting," Samkatt said.

"That's okay. We want them to thaw." Omar turned on the hot water in the kitchen sink. While it ran, he got a glass down from the cupboard. He ran his finger under the faucet to see how hot the water was. Satisfied, he filled the glass.

He pointed to Samkatt. "Drop them in."

"Bombs away!" Samkatt dropped one pinkie and then the other into the glass, splashing water all over the counter. He leaned closer to the glass. "Hey! They float!"

"For now," Omar said. "Once they thaw out, they'll start sinking."

"Now what?" Samkatt said, his eyes fixed on the floating mice.

"We give them twenty minutes." Omar set the timer on the stove to 20. The pinkies definitely looked more mouse-like without ice crystals clinging to them. They were poor dead baby mice who'd never even gotten the chance to open their eyes.

Omar felt his brain running away with him. He had to stop thinking like this. He didn't know how tiny, pink baby mice left the world, and he didn't want to know. Snakes ate mice. If Omar wanted to own a snake, it was his job to provide the mice. End of story.

Samkatt didn't see it that way. He poked the floating pinkies with his finger. "How do you suppose they off these guys?" he asked Omar. "Do they drown 'em? Maybe they just stick 'em in the freezer. That would do it if you left them in there for an hour or so. They don't have any fur to keep them warm."

*Beep... beep... beep!* The timer went off, saving Omar from a topic he didn't want to discuss. "They should be thawed by now," he told Samkatt.

Samkatt poked at the pinkies. He picked one up and pressed its stomach. "Yeah. The water's cooler. They feel mushy inside. I don't think they're frozen anymore."

"Let's do it." Omar took a deep breath. "Oh, wait! Oh, darn!"

"What's the matter?" Samkatt asked, squeezing the second pinkie.

"My dad was supposed to get me a forceps. He was going to bring it home tonight. I didn't think Arrow would be ready to eat yet."

"We can't stop now," Samkatt said. "I bet frozen mice are like frozen burgers. Once they're thawed out, you have to eat them. You can't put them back in the freezer."

"You can leave them in the refrigerator," Omar said.

"Yeah, your mom will really go for that!" Samkatt said. Omar knew he was right. "Why do you need a forceps, anyway?"

"So the snake doesn't mistake your finger for a pinkie."

"Maybe there's something we can use instead of a forceps," Samkatt suggested. "I know! Got any tweezers?"

"Yeah! That would work," Omar said. He rushed to the bathroom. He returned a few minutes later with his mom's eyebrow tweezers.

"Let's do it, dude!" Samkatt said.

"Just one more thing." Omar dug around on the pantry shelf until he found a deep Tupperware container. "This will do."

"What's that for?" Samkatt said.

"Something I learned online. You're not supposed to feed the snake in his habitat," Omar said. "If you do, he'll start associating your hand with food and go for it when you try to pick him up. Also, you don't want to have any of the substrate sticking to the mouse. You don't want the snake swallowing it by accident. Then you have big problems. Also, if the snake gets used to being put in a certain box before he eats, he'll associate that box with being fed. That way, as soon as he goes into the box, he's ready to get down to business."

"So let's US get down to business," Samkatt said. "Can I do the honors?"

"Sure," said Omar. "But we have to wash our hands first. You always wash your hands if you're going to be around snakes." Omar put down the tweezers. He and Samkatt washed their hands in the kitchen sink. Samkatt took the tweezers from the counter. Slowly, carefully, as if he were performing eye surgery, he picked up one of the pinkies by its tail.

"Don't squeeze too tight. The tail might come off," Omar said.

"Relax, dude! Everything's under control," Samkatt said. With the pinkie dangling from the end of the tweezers, he followed Omar upstairs to his bedroom. Omar carried the Tupperware. He set it on the floor in front of his bed. Then he opened the habitat lid. Arrow glided back and forth as Omar turned the dial on the combination lock. Omar saw him stop in the middle of the habitat, raise his head up, and stare.

"He's never done that before," Omar said. "He must be really hungry."

"Dinner is served," Samkatt said, holding up the pinkie. "As soon as that lid comes off, we eat!"

Omar set the lock down on the dresser in front of the habitat to make sure he wouldn't lose it or forget about it. He lowered his face to the habitat's front wall so Arrow could see him. The snake stopped moving back and forth. He raised his head again. Omar could see Arrow's eyes tracking his face.

"What are you doing?" Samkatt said.

"I'm making sure he knows I'm here. I don't want to scare him."

"Dude, that animal would have to be dumber than dirt not to know you're here," Samkatt said. "Like, if a giant lifted up the roof of my house and stuck his face in the window, you think I'd know he was there? Ya think?"

"Bag it," said Omar. "Let me do what I need to do. I'll take care of my end. You take care of yours."

"Hurry up!" Samkatt said. "I don't know how much longer I can hold on to Mousie here. He keeps trying to get away." Samkatt wiggled the pinkie. In a high, squeaky voice he said, "No! No! Don't let that snake eat me! I'm too young to die!"

Omar started feeling annoyed. "Cut it out!" he snapped at Samkatt. "We have to do this right."

"Sorry," Samkatt said. He wiggled the pinkie and squeaked in a Mickey Mouse voice, "Sorry, Omar. I'm ready to do my duty. I only regret that I have but one life to give for my snakey."

Omar could only roll his eyes. All he wanted was a few minutes of quiet so he could concentrate on getting Arrow out of the habitat and into the feeding container. Samkatt finally sat on the bed, holding the tweezers, waiting. He grinned and raised his eyebrows, as if to say, *Okay, I'll stop. Satisfied?*

Omar lowered his hand into the habitat, letting it rest on the substrate, palm up. Arrow glided toward it. Omar felt the slightest tingle as the snake's tongue flicked out to touch his skin. Omar held his breath. The snake glided over his hand. Omar waited until the center of Arrow's body was in the middle of his palm. He closed his fingers around the snake and lifted him out of the habitat.

Omar heard Samkatt whisper, "Awesome!" Keeping a firm grip on Arrow, Omar carried him to the feeder container and gently placed him inside. Arrow glided back and forth. His tongue flicked out every few seconds as he explored this new environment. Not that there was much to explore. But that was the point. There should be nothing in the feeder container to distract the snake from what he was supposed to do. Feed!

"Get ready, Samkatt," Omar said.

Samkatt slipped off the bed and got on his knees. He watched Arrow glide back and forth a few times inside the feeder container. Glancing back over his shoulder, he asked Omar, "He won't bite, will he?"

"I don't know. I never fed him before," Omar said. "I think you'll be okay as long as you keep your fingers out of range."

"Okay, here goes. Let's do it." Samkatt dangled the pinkie in front of Arrow. "Here you go, buddy. Dinnertime."

"He sees it," Omar whispered, standing behind Samkatt and placing a hand on his shoulder. Arrow stopped gliding. His body coiled around itself. His eyes stared straight ahead at the tiny pink lump dangling from Samkatt's tweezers.

"Oh, yeah! He's knows what's up," Samkatt said. "Don't you, buddy? Come on, Arrow. Come get your—"

Suddenly Arrow struck. It happened so fast that Samkatt didn't have time to yelp. The tweezers clattered to the bottom of the feeder container, but neither Omar nor Samkatt paid any attention to them. They kept their eyes riveted to the drama unfolding before them in the plastic container.

Arrow caught the pinkie by the neck. At the same time, he threw a coil around the mouse's body. Omar and Samkatt watched the snake's muscles working, constricting his prey. No energy wasted here, Omar could see. No need to crush the prey. Just keep tightening the coil until it can't breathe. The mouse wasn't breathing anyway. Omar wondered if Arrow could tell that it was dead. Maybe that didn't matter. Omar guessed that snakes were programmed to strike and constrict. They didn't have to go to school. They knew what to do from the moment they hatched.

Arrow released the pinkie. As it lay on the floor of the container, he came around and grasped it by the head.

"Look at that!" Samkatt said. Arrow's jaws opened incredibly wide. He slid his mouth over the pinkie's head as he began swallowing the mouse whole. It was scary yet fascinating to watch as centimeter by centimeter the pinkie disappeared down Arrow's throat. First the head. Then the forelegs. Then the hind legs, until only the tail remained. It stuck out of the corner of Arrow's mouth like a tiny strand of pink spaghetti. Then it, too, disappeared.

Omar and Samkatt watched the lump that had been the pinkie moving slowly down Arrow's body as the snake's swallowing muscles began to work. Neither boy could move.

"Wow!" they both said together.

"Was that ever cool!" Samkatt said. "Okay, Omar. Think you know how to do it? Next one's yours."

"I'll go get it," Omar said. He reached into the container for the tweezers. Despite the lump in his body, Arrow was cruising around. That meant he was still hungry. One more pinkie ought to do it. Omar wondered how long Arrow should be eating pinkies. When was the right time to move him up to the next level, fuzzies? He ought to give the Snake Dude a call sometime next week and ask him about it. *I'll worry about that later,* Omar thought. For now, he needed to feed Arrow the second pinkie and get him back in his habitat so he could finish digesting his meal undisturbed.

"Be back in a flash," Omar said to Samkatt. But Samkatt didn't have a chance to answer. Omar didn't even make it out the door.

Because that was when they heard the scream.

# chapter 14

Footsteps pounded up the stairs. An enraged voice howled, "VERMIN! IN MY HOUSE! IN MY KITCHEN! WAIT TILL I GET MY HANDS ON YOU!"

White-faced, Omar turned to Samkatt. "She'll kill me!" He threw himself against the bedroom door just as his mom arrived.

"Omar! Open this door NOW!"

"Help me, Samkatt! She'll murder me!" Omar begged.

Samkatt didn't move from the floor. "No she won't, dude. Your mom is a nice lady."

"You've never seen her mad," Omar said, bracing his shoulder against the door.

*BANG! BANG! BANG!* Mom pounded on the door with her fist. "Omar! Can you hear me? I'm going to count to three. If this door isn't open...ONE...TWO..."

Omar opened the door. "Hi, Mrs. C-K!" Samkatt said.

Mom looked surprised. "Philip? I didn't know you were here. I'm sorry you had to hear that. I think you'd better go home now. Omar and I need to have a little...TALK!" She glared at Omar with a look that could have melted steel.

"Okay. Bye, Omar. See you around."

Omar mouthed the words *Don't leave me!* Samkatt sighed, as if to say, *What can I do?* "Bye, Omar. Bye, Mrs. C-K," he said as he left the bedroom. Omar heard his footsteps fading away down the hall.

Mom stood in the doorway with her fists on her hips, her foot tapping on the threshold. Omar remembered watching a TV special about King Henry VIII, who chopped off his wife's head. Omar remembered how in the special, soldiers played drums while the executioners led the queen to the chopping block. His mom's tapping foot sounded like those drums. And the look on her face was the same one that was on the king's. It meant: *Expect no mercy.*

"Well? What do you have to say for yourself?"

"Mom, I can explain—" Omar began, his voice breaking.

Mom cut him off before he got the words out of his mouth. "No! Not another word! Nothing you can say is going to get you out of this. You just wait, Omar! Wait till your father gets home! And when he does"—she pointed across the room to the habitat on Omar's dresser—"THAT is going!

"And now," she said, "I'm going to pick up Zara from day care. Make sure that THING is out of MY kitchen when I get back." That wasn't the worst of it. Mom leaned down so that her nose was inches from Omar's face. He could see the powder on her cheeks, the mascara on her eyelashes, the lipstick on her lips. The Bride of Frankenstein could not have been more terrifying. She grabbed Omar by his shirt collar and pulled him even closer. "And I don't want that glass in MY cupboard or in MY dishwasher. You're to throw it in the GARBAGE. Understand?"

"Yes, ma'am," Omar squeaked.

"UNDERSTAND?"

Omar was too frightened to answer. He could manage only a helpless nod.

"I'll talk to you when I get home. We're not done with this. Not by any means."

She slammed the door with a bang and went down the hallway, muttering in Arabic. Omar's class picture from when he was in kindergarten fell off the wall. Omar felt his legs giving way. He reached for the bed, missed, and fell to the floor with a thump. Mom was going to make him get rid of Arrow. And there was nothing he could do about it.

Arrow! Omar suddenly remembered his snake. Poor Arrow must be terrified. All he wanted to do was find a snug, quiet place to digest his meal, and all of a sudden there was this awful yelling and banging. *My gosh! I hope he didn't throw up that pinkie!*

That would be a real mess! Omar jumped up from the carpet and went to his dresser to check. The habitat was empty. Where was Arrow? Then Omar remembered. Arrow wasn't in the habitat. Omar and Samkatt had taken him out to feed him. Arrow had been in the feeder container, having just swallowed the pinkie, when Mom came storming upstairs.

Feeder container? Omar felt his stomach do a nose dive, as if he were in an elevator that had dropped twenty floors in five seconds. He and Samkatt had left Arrow in the uncovered plastic box. Omar suddenly remembered what he had read online about corn snakes being escape artists. If the hole is big enough for the snake to get his head through, he's gone.

Omar closed his eyes and tried to think positive thoughts. If Dad could conjure up parking spaces with positive thinking, maybe he could conjure up Arrow in the feeder container.

*Please, please, please! He ate the mouse. He's tired. He doesn't feel like going anywhere. All he wants to do is sleep. Let him be in the feeder. Please, please, please!*

Omar looked down at the container. He saw exactly what he knew he'd see.

The container was empty.

*Okay, don't panic,* Omar told himself. Arrow couldn't have gone far. Omar looked under his bed, under his dresser, in his closet, behind the clothes hamper, in back of the bookshelf.

He looked everywhere in his room where he thought a snake might hide. Nothing.

"Arrow, where are you?" Omar called in desperation. "I have to find you before Mom gets home!" He sat down on the bed and looked all around the room. Was there a place he might have missed? Arrow had to be somewhere in the room. He couldn't have gotten out.

Or could he? Omar suddenly noticed the crack at the bottom of his bedroom door. There was half an inch between the door and the carpet. More than enough for a snake to glide through. Omar suddenly felt sick.

His snake could be anywhere in the house. Maybe in the bathroom! Omar tuned pale with horror, imagining Mom sitting on the toilet or getting out of the shower when a snake suddenly came gliding out from behind the sink. Something like that would probably win first prize on *America's Funniest Home Videos*. However, it wouldn't be funny at all in real life. If Mom didn't keel over from a heart attack, she'd probably kill the snake. Then she'd kill Omar.

Omar had to find Arrow before Mom did. But how?

Omar felt his desperation growing. He didn't know what to do. But there was someone who might. The Snake Dude! If anyone knew how to find an escaped snake, he was the man.

Omar glanced at the iPod clock radio beside his bed. Four-thirty. That meant he had about a half hour before Mom came home with Zara. He needed to contact the Snake Dude fast. Should he send an e-mail? Then he remembered the Snake Dude giving Dad a business card just before they left. Dad had passed it to him. Where did he put it?

Omar rummaged through his desk. He found the Snake Dude's card pushed to the back of the top drawer. He read the phone number on it. Omar got out his cell phone. He punched in the numbers.

He heard a phone ringing on the other end. *Please, please*

*pick up! Please be there!* After what seemed like forever, Omar heard a familiar voice speaking.

"Yo, Snake Dude speaking. What can I do for you?"

"Uh, Snake Dude? This is Omar. Remember me? I came to your house with my dad on Saturday. You sold us your rescue snake, Alger."

"Sure, Omar! I remember you," the Snake Dude said. "How are things going? You sound like you have a problem."

"Yeah, I do, Snake Dude," Omar said. "It's a big problem. Arrow...I mean Alger...got loose. I've looked all over. I can't find him. I don't know what to do." Omar felt himself gasping for breath. He was trying hard not to cry, but he didn't feel he was winning the battle.

The Snake Dude seemed to understand exactly what Omar was going through. He spoke in a low, calm voice. "Take it easy, Omar. I won't say this isn't serious, but I will tell you that you're not the first person in the world to have a snake escape on him. I've lost dozens over the years. Every snake collector will tell you the same. It happens. The good news is that Arrow...is that what you're calling him? Well, Arrow probably didn't go far. He's somewhere in your house. Would you like me to come over to help you look?"

"NO!" Omar said.

"Gosh! Do I have bad breath or something?" Omar heard the Snake Dude laughing on the other end of the line.

"No, it's not that. I'm sorry." Omar tried to explain. He worried that he was turning off the one person who could help him. "It's just that I can't have you anywhere near the house. Not while my mom's here. She doesn't know Arrow is loose. If she finds out, she'll freak!"

"Gotcha, dude. Okay, I get the picture. Big galoot with a red beard shows up at the door. 'Scuse me, ma'am. I just dropped by to help your boy find the snake that's loose in your house.' Say no more, Omar. Message received. So let me give you some hints that may make finding Arrow easier."

"Anything you can tell me will help," Omar said. He grabbed a pencil and pad from his desk to write down whatever the Snake Dude told him.

"You have to think like a snake to find a snake," the Snake Dude began. "Have you fed him yet?"

"Yeah, I just did. About a half hour ago. He ate one pinkie. My friend and I were going to give him another, but Mom came home first."

"I would have waited a couple more days before feeding him. But if he ate a pinkie, that means he was hungry and feeling comfortable in his new home. No harm there," the Snake Dude replied. "Now if he's just eaten, he's not going to be traveling far. He's going to look for a hide. Some tight, narrow, enclosed space where he can lie low for a couple of days and digest his meal. Look in shoes, drawers, boxes. Remember, a snake can squeeze himself into places you'd think he can't possibly fit in. So look everywhere."

Omar jotted down, "Check tight spaces." The Snake Dude continued.

"A snake would rather be warm than fed. He'd also rather feel secure than warm. So don't assume Arrow will come out looking for food when he gets hungry. He might. Or he might not. I knew a snake that curled up in a shoe and died there. They'll just stay where they are, without food or water, until their life processes start shutting down. It's a kind of hibernation, except they don't wake up."

Omar wrote, "shoe." So far the Snake Dude hadn't told him anything that gave him much hope. Nothing except "Keep looking."

"Isn't there anything else I can do?" Omar asked.

"Yeah," the Snake Dude said. "Your ace in the hole—if you have any aces at all—is the habitat. Arrow's gotten used to it, from what you tell me. He considers it his home. If nothing else, he feels warm and safe in there. So here's what you do. At night, before you go to bed, put the habitat on the floor of your bedroom. Leave the lid open. Make sure the heat mat is plugged in. Fill the water dish with fresh water. If you're lucky, Arrow will come out at night after the house is quiet. Fill another dish with water and put it near the habitat. Also, stack up some books or something next to it so he has an easy way to get in. My guess is he's not going to be moving around much over the next two days. After that, if he goes cruising, looking for a warm place where he feels secure, the habitat just might fill the bill. He'll go inside and curl up in one of the hides. With luck, he'll still be there in the morning when you wake up."

For the first time, Omar could see some light at the end of his long, long tunnel. "Thanks a lot, Snake Dude!" he said.

"Don't thank me yet," the Snake Dude said. "Sometimes it works. Sometimes it doesn't. In the meantime, keep looking. Snakes turn up where you least expect them."

Like in the bathroom when you're getting out of the shower. Omar imagined hearing his mom's scream.

"Thanks for the advice, Snake Dude. I'll try my best," he said.

"Call me anytime. If you want me to come out to help you look, just let me know."

"Thanks."

"Don't mention it." Omar heard the line disconnect. He was about to start searching through his chest of drawers again when he heard the automatic garage door opening, followed a few minutes later by Zara's voice yelling up the stairs.

"Hi, Omar! I'm coming up. I want to see the snake!"

# chapter 15

Now what? Omar felt like a possum trying to cross the freeway. He saw headlights bearing down on him no matter which way he turned. *THINK!* he told himself.

If he let Zara look in the habitat, it wouldn't take her ten seconds to figure out that Arrow wasn't there. Then she'd tell Mom, and Mom would find out the snake was loose. Mom would kill him. But if he didn't let Zara into his room, she'd blab to Mom, and Mom would want to know why he was being such a mean brother and wouldn't let Zara in to see his snake, and Omar would have to tell her why.

And THEN she'd kill him.

Busted either way. Omar wondered if his mom would let him have a last meal before she killed him. Those guys in prison always got to have a last meal. Mom wouldn't have to cook it herself. It would be okay if she let him order something from takeout. Thai food would be nice.

Having resigned himself to his doom, Omar didn't bother to keep Zara out. "Hi, Omar! Where's Arrow?" she chirped as she came bouncing into his bedroom.

"In the habitat," Omar said. He pointed to his dresser.

Zara stood on her tiptoes to see. She looked toward the right, then the left. She went around the dresser to peer in through the sides. "He's not here," she said, looking over her shoulder at Omar.

A sudden idea flashed through Omar's mind. He answered cheerfully, "He's there, all right. You just can't see him."

"Why not?" Zara asked.

"Um...why not?" Omar thought for a minute. "You see... um...Arrow is shedding his skin. When snakes shed their skin, they disappear. You can't see them while their skin is shed. After their skin grows back, you can see them again."

Zara looked into the habitat. Then at Omar. Then back at the habitat again. She went around and around, looking in from the sides as well as the front. Finally, she turned to Omar.

"But you could still see him even without his skin. You could see his insides, right?"

*Good question,* Omar thought. Now he needed to come up with a good answer. He began slowly.

"That's true. But you know how it is. Snakes are embarrassed to have people see them without their skins. Would you want people to see you without your clothes?"

Omar watched Zara considering that. "You see me without clothes. When I take a bath," she said. "Mommy sees me without clothes. Daddy, too."

"Okay, but what about the kids at day care?" Omar asked her. "What if you had to go to day care without your clothes on?"

"No!" Zara shrieked. Then she started to laugh. "No! No! No!" She threw herself on Omar's bed and rolled back and forth, gleefully yelling, "No! No! No!"

"That's how it is with Arrow," Omar explained. "He doesn't want us to see him without his skin. So he hides."

Zara stopped laughing and rolling on the bed. She suddenly became serious. "Where does he hide?"

Mistake! He should have just said Arrow disappeared and left it at that. Zara would have gone for it. "Um...uh...he hides on the bottom. In the substrate," he said. "You know...that curly wood stuff?"

Zara jumped off the bed. She ran back to the habitat. She walked around the dresser again, checking the aspen shavings. "I don't see him."

"I know," Omar said. "I can't, either. He's in the middle. He's way down at the bottom. He has all the wood shavings on top of him. He doesn't want anyone to see him until his skin grows back."

That answer appeared to work. Zara nodded. She turned back to the habitat. "It's okay, Arrow," she said. "I'll let you hide." Then she ran out of the room.

"Mom! Guess what?" she hollered down the stairs.

Omar heard his mom answer, "What?"

"Omar's snake. Arrow. He's hiding because he doesn't have any skin."

"That's nice, dear. You don't need to fool around with that nasty snake. Come down here and wash your hands. I'll get your snack ready."

"He's not nasty. He's nice," Zara said. She looked back at Omar standing in the doorway and grinned.

"Thanks, Zara. I think you're nice, too," said Omar.

"Will you tell me when Arrow gets his new skin so I can come back and see him?" Zara said.

Omar nodded. "Sure. I promise."

Zara went hopping down the stairs, leaving Omar alone to face his main problem. Where was Arrow?

That was when he heard his cell phone beeping. He had a text message. Omar hit the Message button.

DUDE. U OK? CALL ME.

Omar punched in Samkatt's number. He heard two rings before Samkatt answered.

"Hey! You still alive?" Samkatt asked.

"For now. Would I be calling you if I was dead?"

"Good point, dude," Samkatt said. "Say, you ought to thank me. I saved your butt."

"How?" Omar asked.

"Well, when I was leaving, I made a little stop in your garage," Samkatt said. "I took a little package out of your freezer and brought it home."

"The pinkies?"

"No, dude, the broccoli. Of course, the pinkies!"

"Where are they now?"

"In my freezer. Way at the bottom. Nobody's going to find them. And just in case someone does," Samkatt said, "I drew a skull and crossbones on the lid with Magic Marker and wrote 'Samkatt's Special Oil Pencils. Do Not Mess With on Pain of Death.'"

"Do you keep oil pencils in a freezer?" Omar asked. He didn't know much about art.

"No, dude!" Samkatt started laughing. "I don't even know if there is such a thing as oil pencils. It doesn't matter. I've trained everybody in my house not to mess with my art supplies. If they think it's mine, they'll leave it alone. Anyway, we've got worse stuff in our freezer than frozen mice."

"Like what?" Omar asked.

"You don't want to know," Samkatt said. Omar wondered if he was being serious or just being Samkatt. It didn't matter. Samkatt had truly saved Omar's butt by getting the pinkies out of the house before his mom could find them. And that wasn't all. Omar listened as Samkatt continued.

"I've got it all figured out how we're gonna solve the problem of feeding Alger."

"His name's Arrow," Omar said.

"Whatever," Samkatt said. "You can keep the pinkies at my house. I'll tell your mom I want to take her up on her offer to give me drawing lessons. I've been thinking about that. I could learn a lot from your mom. So when it's snake feeding time, I'll bring the frozen mice over to your house and pass them to you. You can feed Arrow while your mom's teaching me. No yelling, no screaming, no little pink uglies floating around on the kitchen counter. All you have to do is slip 'em to the snake so he can live long and prosper. Take a bow, Samkatt! Am I cool or what?"

Omar had to admit that Samkatt was the coolest, smartest kid he'd ever known in his life, besides being the best friend he could ever have. Life was good, except for one slight problem.

"Right now I don't have to worry about feeding Arrow. He's gone," Omar whispered. He didn't want anyone who might be passing in the hallway to hear.

"What?"

"We forgot to put the lid back on the feeder container when my mom was pounding on the door. He got out while we were distracted. Now I can't find him."

"Dude, you've got to find him. Before your mom does," Samkatt said.

"I know." Omar was back where he started. Arrow was gone and he didn't have a clue how to get him back. "I don't know what to do," he said. "I called the Snake Dude at the place where I got Arrow. He gave me some good suggestions, but I don't know. I'm beginning to think finding an escaped snake is not going to be easy."

A shriek from downstairs cut Omar and Samkatt's conversation short. "Omar! STOP whatever you're doing! Come down here THIS SECOND and get this HORROR out of MY KITCHEN! RIGHT NOW!"

The pinkie! He'd forgotten to remove it. But this could work in his favor. "Bye, Samkatt! Gotta go," Omar said. He raced downstairs. "Sorry, Mom. Sorry. Sorry," he murmured. His mom's cold gaze and tapping foot sped him on his way. He scooped the drinking glass from the counter and carried it into the garage. But he didn't dump it in the trash. He hid it under his shirt and carried it up to his room. Later, when his mom wasn't looking, he went down to the kitchen and filled the glass with ice. He carried the glass with the wet, squishy, tiny dead mouse back upstairs.

"Don't worry, Baby Mouse. I have plans for you."

# chapter 16

Dinner was tense, to say the least. Mom ladled out the tuna casserole like an army cook slinging chow in a mess hall. She clumped a serving on Omar's plate and shoved it at him. Zara started whining that she wanted chicken strips. One look from Mom quieted her down.

Omar's dad observed the situation in silence. Finally, he asked, "Would someone please tell me what's wrong?"

"Tell him, Omar!" Mom snapped.

Omar put down his fork. He wasn't hungry at all. All he'd done was move bits of tuna casserole from one side of his plate to the other. Confessing would be a relief. Might as well get it over with. "I left a pinkie mouse in a glass on the kitchen counter," he told his dad. "Samkatt and I were feeding Arrow for the first time. I messed up. I admit it."

"Your son brought vermin into my house!" Mom said. "He broke his promise. The snake has to go."

"No!" Zara shouted. An ice-cold look from Mom put her in her place.

Dad pushed his chair back from the table. "Omar, what do you have to say for yourself?"

"I was only—"

"That's enough. No excuses," Dad said. "We all agreed to follow certain rules. The snake and everything connected with it were to stay in your room. You messed up. Big-time! Mice have no place in the kitchen. Your mom has a right to be angry. If she says the snake has to go, he goes. It's up to your mom."

"Mom, please! Give me another chance! I'll do better. I promise." Omar didn't know what it would take to convince her. All he knew was that he had to do it. Because if he had to take his snake back to the Snake Dude, he'd have to admit to his parents that he no longer had his snake. The fallout from that would be infinitely worse than leaving a pinkie on the kitchen counter.

He got down on his knees and started pleading. "Mom... please... I'm so sorry. Give me another chance...." He heard Zara crying. Then HE started crying.

"Please, Mom... please..."

"Stop! I can't stand it. Omar, get up!"

Omar slipped back into his chair while Dad comforted Zara. Mom glared at him, stone-faced. Omar pulled his eyes away. He stared at the salt shaker, awaiting his doom.

"You can keep your snake."

"Huh?" Had Mom really said that?

"You can keep your snake," Mom repeated. "I'm still angry. You broke the rules and there's no excuse for it. On the other hand, I'm willing to accept that you and Philip were so eager to feed that snake that you didn't take time to think about how you were going to do it. I'll give you a pass this time. But just once. If it happens again, that snake is gone."

Omar couldn't believe what he was hearing. Saved! He wiped his nose and eyes with his sleeve. "Thanks, Mom."

"Don't thank me yet. We still have things to talk about. The kitchen is off-limits to anything having to do with that snake. There will be no mice in the kitchen. No utensil used to prepare our food will be used to feed mice to your snake. You will get your own equipment and maintain it yourself. In other words, Omar, no sticking anything that's been in contact with your snake in the dishwasher or leaving it on the kitchen countertop or in the sink. Understand?"

Omar gulped. "Yes."

"One more thing. Are there any more mice?"

"Y-yes," Omar stammered.

"Where are they? They'd better not be in the freezer. I'm going to check."

"No. They're not. They're at Samkatt's house."

"And Philip's parents have agreed to that?" Mom sounded extremely skeptical.

"That's what he told me," Omar said. "I guess it's true. If it's not, I'll have to find another place to keep them. No matter where they end up, they won't be in your freezer, Mom. I'm sorry about what happened this afternoon. I promise it won't happen again. Honest!"

Omar could see his mom softening. She was still angry. No doubt about that. But at least her anger wasn't white-hot anymore. It was sort of lukewarm. Like the hot water in the drinking glass after the pinkies had been thawing in it.

He was starting to believe that everything was going to work out okay when Zara suddenly announced, "Arrow isn't in his cage anymore."

Mom gasped. "What? Where is he? Don't tell me that snake is loose in the house." She turned to Omar. "Well?" She looked moments away from screaming.

Omar started to laugh. It was a good way to calm his mom down. It was also a good way to buy time. "No, Mom. No. You've got it all wrong. Everything's cool. Arrow didn't escape. He's still in his habitat. What Zara means is you can't see him."

"Why can't you see him?" Mom asked. Omar could hear a foot tapping on the floor. He didn't dare look her in the eye. Instead, he turned toward Zara.

"Tell her, Zara. Tell Mom what I told you."

He didn't have to urge Zara to let it all out. She loved being the center of attention. The words tumbled out in a rush. "Arrow's skin came off. He's invisible till he grows his skin back. That's why nobody can see him. He doesn't want to go to school without his clothes on."

Zara went on for several more minutes. Not much of what she said made sense, but the more she talked, the more Omar could see his mom relax. His dad listened patiently, as he always did. When Zara finished, he looked across the table at Omar and asked, "Is Arrow shedding his skin?"

"Yes," said Omar. "At least, I think so." He tried to remember everything he had read online about what happens when snakes go through a shed. "His eyes were starting to look a little milky."

"That explains everything," Dad said. "Zara's trying to tell us that Arrow is going to shed his skin. When snakes do that, they hide so that their enemies can't see them. We'll just leave Arrow alone until he finishes his shed. Then he'll have a beautiful new skin to show us. Isn't that right, Zara?"

"And Mommy will draw a picture of him. Like the one she's making now," Zara said.

"Yes," Mom said. Omar couldn't be sure what that meant. He doubted his mom would be using Arrow as a model. Maybe it just meant that she was relieved to know that Arrow was still locked in his habitat.

For a moment, Omar saw himself in a famous painting his mom had once showed him. The painting was called *The Gulf Stream*. An African sailor lay on the deck of a wrecked boat. A hurricane had blown down the mast, and it was drifting with the current. Sharks circled the boat. In the distance, a waterspout was coming the sailor's way. Omar felt just like that shipwrecked sailor. He'd survived the hurricane at the dinner table with Zara blabbing away. He still had to face the sharks and the waterspout. Until Arrow was in his habitat, Omar was adrift like that sailor, still lost at sea.

On the other hand, dinner wasn't a complete failure. Omar

finally felt like eating, and a tuna casserole, while not exactly a double-cheese and pepperoni pizza, wasn't all bad. Omar's mom took Zara upstairs to the studio for some mom-daughter quality art time. Omar's heart was in his throat the whole while, as he wondered if they'd run into a snake on the stairs or in the hallway. Or worse—coiled up on top of his mom's easel. He waited for the scream that would indicate his life was over.

It never came. So far, so good. As long as Arrow stayed out of sight, digesting his pinkie, Omar still had a chance to find him before the whole house got into an uproar.

Omar helped his dad put the leftovers away. Omar carried the dishes in from the dining room and stacked them on the counter. Omar's dad did the rinsing. Omar loaded them into the dishwasher.

"So," Dad said, "you came out of that pretty well. You know, Omar, despite everything, your mom loves you very much and would do anything to make you happy."

"I know," Omar said. He took a long time placing the casserole dish on the bottom rack of the dishwasher. His dad was pretty sharp. How much did he know about what was really going on, and how much could he figure out?

"So Arrow's going through a shed?"

"Yeah," Omar said. "I guess he'll start coming out again when his skin gets ready to come off."

"That will be interesting to watch," Dad said. "How was his appetite when you fed him that pinkie?"

"Pretty good," said Omar. "Samkatt just dangled it in front of him and WHAM! He grabbed it just like that!" Omar suddenly remembered the tweezers. Darn! They were still in his room. He had to get them cleaned off and back in the bathroom cabinet before his mom went looking for them.

"Pretty good?" Dad said as he handed Omar the water glasses one at a time. "You know, I've gone online a couple of times to learn more about corn snakes. Do you know what I discovered?"

"What?" Omar said.

"Snakes stop eating before they shed. They go into hiding. They don't come gliding around, looking for food."

"Oh," said Omar, as if he'd suddenly learned a new and interesting fact on The History Channel.

"So I wouldn't say that a snake capable of eating two pinkies was going to shed," Dad continued. "Especially since the data card on Arrow's habitat at the Snake Dude's house noted that he went through a shed a couple of weeks ago. He isn't due for another for at least a month."

"Oh," Omar said again. He desperately needed to come up with a clever answer that would explain everything. Instead, his mind was as flat and blank as one of the dinner plates.

"So what's really going on?" Dad asked.

Omar considered his options as he stacked up the plates. He could run away. But where would he go? He doubted the army would take a fourth grader. And running away would mean abandoning Arrow to die in some dark, forgotten corner of the house, which would make Omar as bad as that doofus Ray.

He could lie. But he'd learned over the years that it never paid to lie to his dad. Dad would just keep on asking questions until he got Omar tied in knots.

That left only one choice. Tell the truth.

Omar measured a teaspoon of dishwasher detergent into the soap container. He closed the dishwasher, locked it, and set it for the energy-saving cycle. Then he pushed the On button. The noise of the dishwasher would hide their conversation from anyone who might be listening. "If I tell you, will you tell Mom?" Omar asked.

"That depends," Dad said. "If your health or safety were involved, I'd have to tell her. If you told me you were doing drugs or had joined a gang, I'd have to take action. Those aren't the kinds of secrets a parent can keep."

"It's nothing like that, Dad," Omar said.

Omar's dad let loose a big sigh. "Good! You had me worried."

"Arrow got loose," Omar said.

"You're kidding!" Dad exclaimed.

"I'm not," Omar said. "I wish I were. He escaped when we had him in the feeder container. We had just fed him the first pinkie when Mom came home. She started pounding on the door, yelling about the pinkie in the kitchen. Samkatt and I got distracted. And Arrow escaped."

"You've got to find him." The gentle smile disappeared from Dad's face. He looked serious, even grim. "If it were just you and me, or even Zara, it wouldn't be a problem. We'd move the furniture, empty drawers and closets, search everywhere until we found him. The problem isn't Arrow. It's your mom. She has a phobia, Omar. A paralyzing fear of snakes. The scientific name is 'ophidiophobia.' She's working hard to overcome her fear, just for you. You must understand that even being in the same house with a snake is a huge step for her. If your mom ran into Arrow in the hallway or in our bedroom or anywhere in the house, I'm afraid she'd have a panic attack. Or worse."

Omar's dad didn't have to describe what "or worse" meant. Omar flashed on a picture of his mom lying facedown in the hallway, with Arrow coiled on her back. "But if she's so scared of snakes, how come she's putting one in that picture she's painting in her studio?"

"That's different," Dad said. "It's not a real snake. Also, she's in complete control. She's the artist. She creates it. The snake does what she wants it to do. If she doesn't like it, she paints over it. Real snakes are different. Nobody controls them."

"What can I do, Dad?" Omar said. "How can I look for Arrow without Mom knowing I'm looking for Arrow?"

"That's a good question, Omar," Dad said as he wiped off the kitchen counter. "Let's sleep on it and see if we can come up with something. I hope we can. For Arrow's sake..."

"Thanks, Dad," Omar said.

"...and yours."

# chapter 17

Although he didn't reveal it to his dad, Omar already had a plan. With luck, he'd be able to catch Arrow while he was sleeping.

Omar waited until his mom put Zara to bed. Then he went downstairs. His parents were in the den, watching some DVD. Omar guessed it must be romantic, because they were sitting close together on the couch and his mom was crying. That was good. If his mom was weeping over a love story, she wouldn't be nosing around in the kitchen. That would give him time to do what he needed to do.

Omar got a paper cup from the pantry. He filled it with hot water from the tap, then headed back upstairs. His mom saw him go by.

"What's the matter, Omar? Can't sleep?" she asked. "Shall I come upstairs and read to you?"

Omar stopped in his tracks. "That's okay, Mom. I just came down to make some mint tea. You watch the movie."

"We've seen it a thousand times," his dad said. "The couple finally gets married, but the bride gets sick and dies. Then the two families who hate each other come to the funeral and become friends. It ends with everybody singing and dancing. Pure Bollywood!"

"Never mind, Omar," Mom said. "It's a great film. It always makes me cry."

"Me, too," his dad said.

"Good night," said Omar. He carried the hot water up the stairs to his bedroom. The glass of ice was still in his desk drawer. The ice had long since melted, but the water still felt cold enough to keep the pinkie from going bad. Omar hoped so, anyway. A snake would throw up a bad pinkie. If a thawed pinkie mouse in a glass on the kitchen counter was bad, a half-digested one on the living room carpet was infinitely worse.

Omar felt sure that the pinkie must be completely thawed by now. Just to make sure, he pressed its abdomen between his fingers. It felt soft and slightly rubbery, like cold pasta. He remembered how repulsed he had felt the first time he had done this. Now, to his surprise, it didn't bother him at all. That was a good sign, considering what he planned to do.

Omar dropped the pinkie into the hot water to warm it up. He waited until his iPod radio alarm clock counted off ten minutes. Then he took out the pinkie and dried it with one of his T-shirts. He decided to try a hint he had picked up at an online site for people who had pet snakes. Cutting open the mouse's head was a good way to get a snake to eat. The mixture of blood and brains stimulated the snake's appetite. Omar had been totally grossed out when he read that. Now he was running out of options. Using the scissors on the Swiss Army knife his dad had given him for his birthday last year, he snipped open the pinkie's head. Blood and icky stuff squirted out. Omar had worried that he might throw up. It turned out to be not too bad. Unpleasant, but not really horrible.

"I guess people who keep snakes for pets get used to anything," he told himself. That was certainly happening with him.

Now to carry out the plan. Omar set aside the T-shirt and the pinkie. He emptied the water from the paper cup into the glass. Then he used the Swiss Army scissors to cut away the cup's sides to make a little round tray. Next, he moved the habitat from the top of the dresser to the floor of his bedroom. He placed it about two feet from his bed. That was as far as he could go and still keep the heat mat's cord plugged in.

Omar opened the lid and set the cup bottom holding the pinkie on the substrate, on the warm side of the habitat. He used books and dirty clothes to create a gently sloping ramp leading from the floor to the top of the habitat. The idea was that Arrow would come out to explore after the house got quiet. The smell of the warmed-up pinkie would lure him into the bedroom. He'd glide up the ramp and back into his old habitat, where there were food, water, warmth, and good places to hide. What more could a snake ask for? After swallowing the pinkie, he'd coil up in the toilet paper tube or maybe the cereal box. With luck, he'd be there in the morning when Omar got up. Omar would just have to close the lid, lock it, and put the habitat back on his dresser. Problem solved!

That was the theory. However, as Dad often pointed out, history was full of great theories that didn't work. *No, it will work,* Omar thought as he emptied the glass in the bathroom sink and washed his hands. *It has to work!*

Omar had no sooner closed his eyes than he heard the alarm going off. Six o'clock! He heard the shower running and smelled fresh coffee brewing downstairs in the kitchen. Where had the night gone? Omar had wanted to be awake when Arrow came through the door. Too late for that. What about the rest of the plan. Had it worked?

Omar rolled to the edge of his bed. He leaned over to look into the habitat. Did he see what he thought he saw? Yes! Omar felt like jumping up and pumping his fist into the air. The paper-cup tray was empty! Arrow had come in the night. He'd taken the pinkie. He'd gone into the habitat. With luck, he'd still be there.

But Omar's luck had run out. He looked in the hides. He

looked in and behind the water dish. He combed his fingers through the substrate in case Arrow had burrowed under the aspen. Nothing!

Arrow had glided in, swallowed the pinkie, and glided out. How had he gotten out? Omar hadn't thought Arrow was long enough to reach the top of the habitat from inside. He realized he'd been wrong about that. Where a snake's head can go, the rest of its body will follow.

If only he'd hadn't fallen asleep! Omar was back where he started, except this time Arrow had two pinkies to digest. He was happily hidden somewhere. He wouldn't be coming out of his hide—wherever and whatever it was—for days. No time to look for him now. Omar had to get ready for school.

Omar sat in his seat, chewing on the end of his pencil. He tried hard to think of a time when he had been bullied, so he could raise his hand, too. So far, he'd come up blank. That surprised him, since just about every other kid in the class stood up to tell about how he or she had been bullied. Except it seemed to Omar that a lot of his classmates were really stretching it.

If someone bumped into you, that was bullying.

If someone cut in front of you in line, that was bullying.

If someone yelled at you or looked at you funny, that was bullying, too.

It seemed to Omar that most of his classmates liked being bullied. Or at least, they liked saying that they'd been bullied so Ms. Ortiz would ask, "How did that make you feel?" Then they'd go on and on about their feelings.

Omar could recall being bullied only once, and it hadn't amounted to anything. His mom had made him a Lebanese sandwich for lunch, with pita bread, olives, tomatoes, lettuce, and feta cheese. Another kid said it looked weird, so Omar told his mom to make him peanut butter and jelly from then on. Was that bullying? Maybe, since Mom's Lebanese pita sandwiches tasted a whole lot better than peanut butter and jelly. Omar wished he could be more like Samkatt, who brought all kinds of weird stuff for lunch and ate it with chopsticks. Samkatt didn't care what anybody thought.

Omar wondered if he should raise his hand to tell that story. Before he could make up his mind, Ms. Ortiz began talking about how to deal with bullies. Never fight back. Tell someone right away. Then she started in on how bullies were kids who didn't feel good about themselves. As Omar listened, he found himself beginning to feel sorry for bullies. That seemed strange. Why should anybody feel sorry for people who made other people feel bad?

Omar looked over to see what Samkatt was doing. He was working on one of his samurai cat cartoons. A bully was forcing two little kids to hand over their lunch money. The kids started crying. Then, all of a sudden, the samurai cat appeared. He said to the bully, "I'm sorry you don't feel good about yourself. This will help you feel better." Then he cut off the bully's head with his sword. The last panel showed the samurai cat and the little kids running around on a soccer field, kicking the bully's head back and forth like a soccer ball. They looked like they were having a really good time.

"You'd better cover that up. I don't think the Big O would like it," Omar whispered to Samkatt. "She might send you for counseling."

Samkatt went right on drawing. "She asked how we felt about bullies. This is how I feel about bullies," he whispered back. "What's happening with you?"

"I can't find Arrow. I came close. He came into his habitat at night and ate the second pinkie. I was asleep, so he got right out again."

"Darn!" Samkatt said the word a little too loudly. The Big O turned in his direction. Samkatt looked back at her as if he hadn't said anything. Eventually, she turned back to Evelyn Fletcher, who was saying how we should love everybody because God loves us. Samkatt turned to the next page in his notebook.

He divided it into eight panels, labeling the first one "Evelyn Fletcher Meets the Vampire."

"I don't know what to do," Omar said. "I might be able to find him if I search the rest of the house. But I don't know how to do it without tipping off Mom."

"I have an idea," Samkatt said as he drew a fairly good likeness of Evelyn Fletcher, standing in an alley with her hands together in prayer and her eyes looking upward while a menacing figure crept up behind her from the shadows. "Vacuum."

"What?" Omar asked.

"Offer to vacuum the house. Really vacuum. That will give you an excuse to go into each room and move furniture around."

"Wouldn't the vacuum noise frighten Arrow?" Omar said.

"So?" Samkatt said. "He'll either hunker down or make a run for it. Either way, you grab him."

"Snakes don't run," Omar said.

"Whatever," said Samkatt as the menacing figure popped Evelyn Fletcher into a sack and carried her off to a hilltop mansion labeled "Castle Dracula."

# chapter 18

Omar and Samkatt discussed the plan on the way home from school. The only drawback that Omar could see was that suddenly volunteering to vacuum the whole house would arouse his mom's suspicions.

"What's she got to be suspicious about?" Samkatt said. "She doesn't know Arrow is gone."

"She knows I hate to vacuum," Omar said. "If I suddenly offer to do it, she'll think something is up. You're right. She doesn't know Arrow is gone. But if she gets suspicious, she might start looking around. If she looks around long enough, she may find something."

"If she finds something, your problem is solved," Samkatt said. "You'll know where your snake is. Just listen for the scream."

"Very funny," Omar said.

"I'm serious," Samkatt said. "Look, think about it. This can work. I'll cover for you. I'll tell your mom I'd like her to give me a drawing lesson. While I'm in the studio, you offer to vacuum to make up for the fright you gave her with the mouse. I'll keep her busy so you can keep searching."

Omar had to admit that Samkatt had every angle covered. "Then what are you waiting for? Let's do it."

Samkatt went home with Omar after school. Omar's mom was in the studio. Omar tapped lightly on the door. "Mom, I'm home," he said. "Samkatt's with me."

"Come on in," Mom called from inside.

"Wow!" Omar exclaimed when he saw the painting on the easel.

"Like it?" his mom asked.

"That's pretty cool, Mrs. C-K," Samkatt said.

"Thanks, Philip. What about you, Omar?"

Omar didn't know what to say. The painting was even more bizarre than the first time he'd seen it. The woman in the painting—who still looked very much like his mom—still had a snake. Except now she wasn't holding it. She was dancing with the snake coiled around her body. Her skin now matched the pattern of the snake's skin, so that it was hard to tell the woman's body from the snake's. Omar immediately thought of the Snake Dude and his tattoos. The woman held the snake's head so that the two figures faced each other. Their tongues touched. The woman had a snake's forked tongue. Weird! Omar couldn't help wondering: Was the snake becoming a woman, or was the woman becoming a snake?

"What's it supposed to mean?" Samkatt said.

"What do you think it means?" said Omar's mom.

"I don't know," Samkatt said.

"Well, I don't know, either. I know what it means to me. I can't tell what it means to you."

"But you're the artist," Samkatt said.

Omar knew exactly how his mom would answer. "And you want me to give you the right answer so you don't have to think about it. You want me to do your thinking for you. Sorry, Philip. That's not how art works."

"I still don't get it," Samkatt said.

"You don't have to. Maybe there's nothing to get."

At this point Omar jumped in. Samkatt and his mom could argue about art all day. He needed to get started vacuuming. "Mom," he said, "Samkatt...uh, Philip...he wanted to know if he could start taking drawing lessons with you, like you promised. Do you remember?"

"Of course I remember!" Mom said as she began putting paints away and cleaning her brushes. "I've been wondering if you would ever take me up on it, Philip. I'm ready to start now. What about you?"

"That's great, Mrs. C-K. Thanks for doing this," Samkatt said.

"Don't mention it. I'm glad you're beginning to take your talent seriously."

While his mom hunted around for a drawing pad and a package of artist's charcoal, Omar saw his chance to make his exit. "Mom, I think I'd like to vacuum."

Omar's mom stared back in surprise. "You HATE to vacuum."

"Yeah, I know," Omar said. "But I think I'd like to anyway. To make up for that shock I gave you yesterday with the mice."

"That's thoughtful of you, Omar," his mom said. "If you're willing, I'd better take you up on it. An offer like this doesn't come along every day. Philip and I will be here. Just knock if you need anything."

"I will," Omar said. He caught Samkatt winking at him as he shut the door. Samkatt mouthed the words *Way to go!*

Omar hurried downstairs. He got the vacuum cleaner from the pantry closet and carried it upstairs. Where to start? There was no point in wasting time on his own room. He could search there whenever he wanted. He also had the feeling that if Arrow had been hiding in his room, he would have found him by now. That left two choices: Zara's room and his parents'.

He decided to go with Zara. Her room was smaller, so he expected it wouldn't take as long. Mistake! Zara's room was a jumble of dolls, stuffed animals, picture books, drawing pads, crayons, felt markers, and colored pencils. Not to mention clothes and dress-up costumes, including seven princess tiaras, four sets of fairy wings, two white and three pink ballerina tutus, plus enough magic wands to outfit Hogwarts. The clutter was so overwhelming that Omar had no idea where to begin. More important, the places where a snake might hide were endless. Any search of Zara's room would require an entire weekend. Doable, Omar decided. He and Zara could make it a game. Zara would love the attention.

Omar made a note to plan it for Saturday. He wouldn't mind giving up a day or even a whole weekend if he could get Arrow back in his habitat.

In the meantime, he cleared enough space to get the vacuum into the room and give the carpet a once-over, sucking up crumbs, candy wrappers, and broken crayons. He gathered up all the clothes on the floor and put them in the hamper. Then he moved on down the hall to his parents' room.

This was a different world, with everything prim, neat, and in its proper place. Omar rolled the vacuum inside and shut the door.

He looked under the bed, under the nightstands, under the dressers. Unlike in Zara's room, he had a clear view to the wall. Nothing. He looked in his mom's closet first. Rows of clothing hung on wooden hangers in separate sections, with gowns and business suits zipped up in plastic bags. Each bag had its own label. Shoes were arranged in neat rows on two lower shelves. It was the same in his father's closet. Suits, slacks, shirts, and jeans had their own special places.

Omar looked below and behind, but he couldn't see any place where a snake might hide. It was the same with the dressers and his mom's vanity table. Omar tried thinking like a snake. He lay down on the floor and looked around. Whether he thought like a snake or thought like Omar, he came to the same conclusion.

There was nothing here. His parents' room was too neat, too orderly. There was no nook, cranny, crack, or out-of-the-way refuge to make a snake feel secure. Omar felt certain that Arrow would look around and then move on. Omar moved on, too. He turned on the vacuum to make a noisy show of vacuuming the already immaculate carpet before heading downstairs.

He was almost out the door when he noticed a paperback book on the floor beside his mom's bed. He bent down to put it back on the nightstand. He glanced at the title. *Know Fear/No Fear* by somebody named Dr. Michael S. Klaybor.

What was this about? Omar flipped through the pages. It was a book about phobias and how to overcome them. Omar's mom had underlined several paragraphs. Omar read a few of them.

Having a phobia means being afraid of something that can't hurt you. There are hundreds of phobias, but they all work the same way.

Omar read on. This Dr. Klaybor was a pretty good writer. Omar could pretty much understand what he was saying. He didn't use a lot of big words and long sentences.

According to the book, a scary event when you're a little kid can cause a phobia. Your parents taking you to the mall and forcing you to sit on Santa's lap when you're scared to death of this weird guy in a red suit can give you a lifelong fear of Santas, clowns, or anybody wearing a costume. The way to overcome a phobia is to reverse the process. You set up situations where a frightened person can slowly and gradually get comfortable with whatever it is he's afraid of.

In other words, first you'd look at pictures of Santa. When you got comfortable with that, you might watch a Christmas video with Santa Claus in it. You could rent a Santa costume and lay it on the bed and just look at it. Or try it on. You could go to the mall at Christmas and watch Santa from the upper level.

Gradually, you'd get closer, step by step, until you were sitting on Santa's lap, telling him what you wanted for Christmas.

Omar wondered why Mom was reading about Santa. Then he realized that this had nothing to do with Santa. It was about snakes. That was why his mom was painting that picture of the woman with the snake. Looking at a picture of a snake, painting herself holding a snake, becoming the snake, was her way of trying to overcome her phobia.

And why? Because she knew how much Omar wanted a snake. Omar thought how terrifying it must be for someone with a snake phobia to be living in the same house with a snake. That was what had tipped Mom over the edge on the day Arrow escaped. She might have been angry, but she'd also been very, very scared. And Omar had thought she was just being uptight.

Omar sat down on the bed. He put the book on the nightstand. He felt sad and happy at the same time. Mom must love him an awful lot to try so hard to conquer a fear she must have had since she was a little girl. Omar wondered if he could ever be so brave. At the same time, he felt ashamed for not having tried to understand how his mom must feel and for thinking only about himself. He remembered Dad telling him that Mom had a phobia. At the time, he didn't understand what that meant.

Now he did.

It wasn't fair to ask someone who was afraid of snakes to share a house with one. Omar felt a great sense of peace come over him. He knew what he had to do.

It was time to stop sneaking around. He had to come out and tell the truth. Arrow was loose. He was probably hiding somewhere in the house. Omar would keep searching until the weekend. If he hadn't found Arrow by then, he'd tell his mom. She'd have the choice of staying or leaving while Omar, his dad, and Zara thoroughly searched the house on Saturday and Sunday.

If they found Arrow, Omar would call the Snake Dude and ask him to take Arrow back. He could have Arrow's habitat and everything that went with it. Maybe that would make it easier for someone who really wanted a snake but couldn't afford to buy all the stuff to give Arrow a good home.

Omar still wanted a pet snake someday. He knew he could do a good job of caring for one. Maybe in the future, when he was in college, or grown-up and on his own. But not now.

Omar carried the vacuum downstairs. He went through the living room, dining room, family room, kitchen, and pantry. He searched every object that could possibly be a hide. He opened drawers and closets, looked behind bookcases, poked through the shelves of DVDs in the entertainment center. Nothing.

Now what? Omar vacuumed aimlessly around the living room. The roar of the vacuum cleaner helped him think. Could Arrow have gotten into the garage? Maybe. But the door to the garage was never left open for long. Arrow would have had to slip through unnoticed while someone was either going out or coming in. Omar didn't think there was much chance of that.

On the other hand, if Arrow had gotten into the garage, there were plenty of places to hide. Behind or under the gardening table. Freezer, same. There were also the heavy steel storage shelves and all the boxes stored on them. Not to mention the lawn mower, wheelbarrow, buckets, pails, and Dad's tools. Omar had to admit there was better hiding in the garage than in the house, with less chance of being disturbed. Besides that, the big garage door was usually left open for long periods if the weather was good and someone was home.

*Face it,* Omar thought. *If Arrow made it to the garage, he's gone.*

Another thought came back like an echo: *Find him or not, he's gone either way.*

# chapter 19

Omar vacuumed until Samkatt finished his drawing lesson. Samkatt came down the stairs clutching a large drawing pad and a plastic sandwich bag containing several sticks of drawing charcoal.

"How'd it go?" said Omar as he wound up the vacuum cleaner cord.

"Awesome!" Samkatt said. "Your mom had me draw a ball."

"You spent two hours drawing a ball?" Omar said. "How hard could it be to draw a ball? You make a circle and if you want, you color it in. Zara can draw a ball."

"Dude! It's harder than you think," said Samkatt. "Your mom is teaching me all about shading. You really have to look at the ball to get it right. You have to pay attention to where the light's coming from, how it hits the ball, where the shadows fall. I'll show you."

Samkatt set down the charcoal and opened the drawing pad. The first sheet was filled with shaded balls. Some were shaded on the left, some on the right, some on top. The second sheet had a drawing of one big ball that filled the page. It was shaded on the left. It definitely looked like a round ball and not a circle. If this was what art was all about, Samkatt was getting the hang of it. But Omar couldn't see how drawing balls would bring Samkatt closer to his dream of becoming an anime artist in Japan. Maybe the samurai cats could detonate their enemies with atomic balls.

"Your mom says becoming an artist is about learning how to see," Samkatt said.

"Okay," Omar said. He was glad Samkatt had enjoyed the lesson. As for Omar, the only thing he wanted to see right now was a red-and-orange snake. But he didn't have time to think about that because Mom was coming downstairs.

"Philip and I enjoyed that lesson. Why don't you join us next time?" Mom said to Omar.

"I might," Omar said, "after I get the vacuuming done."

"I never knew you to be so fond of vacuuming. What gives?" his mom asked.

"I just felt like vacuuming," Omar said.

"I won't stand in your way. Tell me if you ever get the urge to mop. Or do windows." She slipped on a jacket and took her purse and car keys. "I'm going to pick up Zara from day care. I can drop you off at your house. It's on the way," she said to Samkatt.

"I'm cool, Mrs. C-K," Samkatt said. "I can walk home. It's not far."

"Anytime, Philip," Omar's mom said. "Let's have another lesson soon. I enjoyed it. See you next week? And keep practicing. I'll want to see what you've drawn."

"Sure, Mrs. C-K. And thanks." Omar's mom disappeared out the door. Omar and Samkatt heard the garage door opening and the car starting up.

"What happened?" Samkatt said. "Did you find anything?"

"Not a trace," Omar said.

"Where'd you look?"

"Everywhere! My room, my parents' room, all over downstairs."

"What about Zara's room? And the garage?" Samkatt said.

"Not today," Omar said, shaking his head. He carried the vacuum back to the pantry closet. "Zara's room is a jungle. And it doesn't pay to look in the garage. If Arrow made it to the garage, he's gone."

"Don't say that," Samkatt said. "I'll come back and help you. You want to try again tomorrow?"

"Maybe," Omar said. "I have some things to do first."

"Like what?"

"Things" was all Omar would say.

Omar waited outside for his dad to get home from work. Dad worked as the chief financial officer of a medical software company in Portland. That meant he was the guy who looked after the money. The company's programs allowed health workers in Third World countries to access medical databases and consult with experts all over the world. "Our business is saving lives," Dad liked to say.

Saving the environment was another issue that was important to Omar's dad. He rode the light-rail system to work. He drove to the park-and-ride in Oregon City and took the train up to Portland. He had to leave a little earlier than if he'd been driving the whole way, and it took a little longer to get home, but he always said it was a small price to pay to keep a beautiful part of the world beautiful. Dad and Mom had gone to college in Southern California. They did not miss smog or bumper-to-bumper freeways.

That was what Omar admired most about his dad. If Dad believed in something, he lived it. He never said one thing and did another. He never told Omar "It's different with grown-ups" or "You'll understand when you're older." Omar could talk to his dad about anything. He knew his dad would always give him a straight answer, even if it wasn't what he wanted to hear.

This evening they had a lot to talk about.

"Any luck?" Dad asked as he drove up the driveway. He stopped the car in front of the garage door.

Omar shook his head. "Samkatt had a really good idea. I'd vacuum while he took a drawing lesson from Mom. I vacuumed upstairs, downstairs. Couldn't find anything."

"You must feel really discouraged about that," Dad said. He pressed the button for the automatic garage door opener.

"Kinda," Omar said. His dad drove the car into the garage. He came out again, ducking under the creaky garage door as it closed behind him.

"Want to take a walk?" he asked Omar. Omar nodded.

Omar and his dad walked around the cul-de-sac. They crossed Steller's Jay Way to the park. They followed the path to the tennis courts, neither one saying anything. Omar spoke first.

"I'm worried that I may not find Arrow."

Dad nodded. "That might happen. I was thinking about that, too. A snake's survival depends on its ability to hide. They've been doing it successfully for millions of years. Humans have been here for only maybe two hundred thousand. With those odds, they've got us beat. Easy."

Omar could tell that his dad was making a joke. He didn't feel like laughing. "Even if I find him," he said, "I don't think I can keep him."

"Why not?" Dad asked.

"It's not fair to Mom," Omar said. "I vacuumed in your bedroom while I was looking for Arrow. I saw that book about phobias she was reading. I never understood how scared Mom was of snakes. It's not fair for me to have a snake. I can't do that to Mom."

They found a bench to sit on. They watched the tennis players. An older man was playing with two teenagers. He looked like a coach or something. The man hit tennis balls and the teenagers tried to hit them back. Omar could tell that the old guy was a pro. He had the kids running all over the court, but he didn't look as if he was raising a sweat. It was fun to watch. It looked a lot more interesting than regular PE.

"I think your mom's okay with a snake. As long as it's in your room in a habitat," Dad finally said.

"But it's not," Omar said. "What if Mom sees it in the hall? Or in the bedroom? That would freak her out. I'm scared she might have a heart attack. Or a stroke. Or something."

"That's a little extreme," Dad replied. "But you're on the right track. She'd certainly be freaked, as you say."

One of the tennis players hit the ball wild. It came soaring over the chain-link fence. "Hey! Could you get the ball?" the old guy called to Omar.

"Sure!" said Omar. He picked up the neon-yellow ball and threw it back over the fence. "Good arm!" the old guy said.

"Thanks," said Omar, sitting back down. He turned to his dad. "I don't want that to happen. Mom has to know what's going on. I have to tell her that Arrow's loose."

"She won't be happy," Dad said.

"I know. I can't help it," Omar said. "I have to tell her. I want to go over the house completely this weekend. Maybe I'll find Arrow. Maybe I won't. At least, I'll know I did my best. And if I do find him, he'll have to go back to the Snake Dude. I can't keep him."

"Are you okay with that?" Dad asked.

"Yeah," Omar said. "I've been doing a lot of thinking about Mom and snakes. It's like if Zara was allergic to peanuts. We couldn't have peanuts or peanut butter in the house. I wouldn't feel sad. Okay, so I can't have a peanut butter sandwich. That's no tragedy. It's just the way it is. I don't want Mom being afraid all the time. I didn't understand that when we got Arrow. But I understand it now. I'll find another pet, Dad. Or maybe I won't have a pet. It's not the worst thing in the world. Maybe I'll take up tennis."

Omar's dad didn't answer. He sat quietly, watching the tennis ball go back and forth over the net. Finally, he reached out and tousled Omar's hair. "You know what, Omar? You're a good kid. I'm glad I'm your dad."

"So am I," Omar said.

Omar knew what he had to do. Now the question was: when to do it? He kept hoping that Arrow would appear and the problem would solve itself. Three days went by before he realized that wasn't going to happen. By then, it was Friday. Tomorrow was Saturday. It would probably be best to just tell Mom that night and get it over with. Maybe at dinner, when the whole family was sitting around the table. Mom would be less likely to lose it in front of Zara. But the more Omar considered that plan, the less he liked it. Mom would have to spend the whole evening in the house, knowing that a snake was loose somewhere. And then she'd have to go to bed. She might close her eyes for five seconds the whole night long! What if she had to go to the bathroom? Omar thought, *If I were scared of snakes, would I get up in the middle of the night to walk down a dark hallway to a dark bathroom where a snake might jump me the moment I sat down?*

Omar crossed off the idea of telling his mom that night. That left the next morning. Early the next morning. Say, around breakfast. That way, if Mom freaked, she could just leave. Go to the mall. Drive up to Portland to visit her friend Jeanne, who had the gallery in the Pearl District. She might take Zara with her. Even better! That would leave him and Dad plenty of time to search the house without Zara pestering them every minute.

*That's the answer,* Omar thought. Tell her at breakfast. Mom and Zara would take off, and by the time they got back, Arrow would either be in his habitat or gone forever.

It was a pretty good plan. And the best part was that Omar couldn't think of any way it could fail.

# chapter 20

It didn't seem to Omar that he slept at all that night. Over and over again in his mind he rehearsed the words he knew he would have to say. "Mom, I have something to tell you.... Mom, I don't want you to get upset.... Mom, there's something you need to know...."

Yet he must have fallen asleep at some point, because suddenly he saw sunlight coming through his window. He rolled over to look at his alarm clock. Seven-thirty. He closed his eyes as he lay back on the pillow, savoring a few extra moments of calm before heading into the hurricane downstairs.

Someone knocked on the door. "Omar? Are you up yet?" It was Dad.

"Yeah. I'm getting dressed." Omar pushed back the covers. He swung his feet onto the floor.

"How are you doing? Did you get any sleep?"

"Yeah. A little. I think."

"Are you ready?"

"Yeah, Dad. I'm okay. I can handle it."

"I know you can," Omar heard his dad say as he walked

down the hall to the stairs. He heard his mom yelling from the kitchen. "Omar! Zara! Time to get up!"

Omar pulled a T-shirt out of his drawer. He stuck his arms through the sleeves and pulled it down over his head. He glanced at himself in the mirror. The shirt had a blue heron on it. He remembered hearing somewhere that blue herons were lucky birds. Lucky if you weren't a frog or a fish. Or a snake, Omar reminded himself. Blue herons ate snakes. Thinking about snakes reminded him to check the habitat. It was still on the floor. He hadn't moved it since the day Arrow escaped. He checked the hides, although he was fairly sure what he would find. Or wouldn't find.

The habitat was empty. There was an extremely remote possibility that Arrow had come into his room at night for water. Omar had been changing the water in the water dish every morning to make sure that Arrow would have fresh water if and when he showed up. Imagining that happening helped Omar feel slightly hopeful.

Given the choice between hopeful and hopeless, Omar decided he would rather feel hopeful. However, after three days without a sign of Arrow, he didn't have much hope left. He pulled on his jeans, buckled his belt, and shoved his feet into running shoes. He didn't bother lacing them. Instead, he unplugged the heat mat and lifted Arrow's habitat back up onto his dresser. Without thinking, he began winding up the cord.

*No, wait!* Omar caught himself as he was about to drop the electric cord into the habitat. *I'm not ready to give up. We may find Arrow. If we do, he'll need to have the right temperature in the habitat.* Omar bent down. He plugged the heat mat's cord into the wall socket. He felt his imaginary needle inch slightly toward hopeful as he shuffled to the hall and down the stairs.

Omar found his mom bustling around the kitchen. "Go sit down. I'll have everything ready in a minute," she said.

Omar looked into the den. He saw Zara dancing around in

her princess outfit. She had a plastic tiara stuck in her hair, a plastic magic wand with blue ribbons on the handle and a blue star on the end, and a pink tutu around her waist. The finishing touch was her lavender Cinderella princess purse, featuring a picture of Cinderella running down a wide staircase with the handsome prince running after her, holding the glass slipper in his hand. Zara sang as she danced, "I am the beautiful princess. I've come to break the spell. Here! Here! Here! Here!" With each "Here!" she touched some invisible person, turning frogs into people or people into frogs or whatever was going on in her head. Omar had to agree with Samkatt. Little kids could be really strange.

"Hi, Zara!" Omar said, waving to her.

"I'm PRINCESS Zara," Zara said. She danced up to Omar. "I have a secret," she whispered.

"Good," Omar said, walking into the kitchen.

"It's a special secret," Zara said. "I know something you don't know," she sang as she danced away.

"Whatever," Omar said to himself.

Dad poured boiling water into the French press to get the coffee going. He turned up the radio to hear whatever the NPR commentators were discussing.

Omar couldn't understand why his dad always started the day with news that was always depressing. A terrorist bomb killed a hundred people. A train wreck killed a hundred people. A boat sank and drowned a hundred people. Omar once asked his dad why the news had to be so depressing. Wasn't there any happy news?

"News isn't supposed to be happy," Dad replied. "If you want to be happy, watch *American Idol*." But even that wasn't happy. All the people who got voted off the show either started crying, or else they started screaming at the judges. Omar felt himself tense at that thought. Soon there was going to be screaming in his house that would make *American Idol* look like *SpongeBob SquarePants*.

He pulled up a chair and sat down next to Zara. "Hi, Omar!" she said. "Did you say hello to Chelsea?" Chelsea was Zara's imaginary friend who showed up from time to time.

"Hi, Zara. Hi, Chelsea," Omar said. "Is there anything I can do, Mom?" he asked.

"No. I've got it. Just sit there and keep Zara happy. That's all the help I need."

It was a bright, sunny morning. No rain. Not a cloud in the sky. And his mom seemed so cheerful. Omar felt himself tense even more. He could feel the countdown beginning. In a few minutes he would bust this happy morning wide open.

Omar's dad sat down with a cup of coffee and the newspaper while his mom loaded the table with plates and bowls. She was serving her famous Peace In The Middle East breakfast: pita, hummus and tahini, olives, thick Lebanese yogurt called *laban,* feta cheese, bagels, cream cheese, and this very expensive, very salty smoked salmon called lox that nobody else but Mom liked.

"Dig in," she said, rushing back to the counter to pour her own cup of coffee. "Zara, shall I toast a bagel for you? Or do you want Cheerios?"

"Cheerios," Zara said. Mom filled a bowl with cereal and milk and brought it to her.

Omar poured himself a glass of orange juice. Zara began slurping away. She flashed a drippy grin at Omar. "I have a secret," she said. "Nobody knows. Just Chelsea and me."

"Cool!" Omar said. He helped himself to olives and cheese. He tore off half a pita, dipping one end into the hummus. Omar's mom came over and sat down. She cut a bagel in half and smeared on a lump of cream cheese, topping it off with a bright-orange slab of lox.

"I have a secret," Zara said again, to no one in particular.

"Oooh! I like secrets," Mom said. She turned to Dad. "What's new in the world besides war, disaster, famine, and pestilence?"

"I'll tell you the good news as soon as I find it," Dad said. He sipped at the scalding-hot coffee in his cup, then turned to the business section of the paper. "The stock market tanked again." He looked across the table at Omar. His eyebrows went up as he stared over the top of his glasses. Dad didn't have to say a word for Omar to get the message he was sending: *Well?*

They were all here at the table. What was he waiting for? Omar braced himself. He sipped some more orange juice, put down the glass, took a deep breath, and said, "Mom, I have something to tell you."

At the same moment, Zara piped up. "I have a secret!"

Mom turned to Zara. "Good! And I want to hear it, dear. But Omar spoke first. Let me listen to him. Then I'll listen to you. I really want to hear your secret." She smiled at Zara, then turned to Omar. "What did you want to tell me?"

Omar felt his nerve slipping away. "Uh, that's okay, Mom. Zara can go first."

"I have a secret!" Zara repeated. She bounced up and down in her booster seat.

"I know, dear. You told me. Is it something you can share or do you want to keep the secret for yourself?" Mom asked.

"I'll tell you," Zara said loudly enough for everyone at the table to hear.

"What is it?" Mom leaned closer. She cupped her hand to her ear, pretending to be listening to a quiet, inside voice.

"I'll show you!" Zara said.

"Good. Show me."

Zara propped her Cinderella purse on the table. "The secret's inside."

"Oooh! Let me see it!"

Omar rolled his eyes. He regretted giving up his turn. Why was it, he wondered, that everything little kids did was always so long and involved?

Zara opened her purse to show Mom the big secret.

What occurred next took only a few seconds. Omar knew that. Yet even as he watched, it seemed that time slowed way down. Everything happened in slow motion.

First, he saw his mom scream, but he couldn't hear a sound. Her eyes went wide. Her mouth flew open. But nothing came out. It was as if he were watching a slasher DVD and somebody hit the Mute button. Then she pushed herself up and away from the table. It seemed as if she were launching herself into space. Her chair tipped backward. Omar saw her falling, falling. Her hands reached out to catch the table, but they caught only the tablecloth. Plates and cups and everything on them went flying as Mom hit the wall behind her.

Omar saw her head strike hard. There should have been a loud *THWACK!* Omar heard nothing. He saw his mom's eyes roll up into their sockets as she slid down the wall into a soggy mess of milk, coffee, orange juice, olives, pita, and bagels. Dad was out of his chair immediately, yelling something at Omar. But Omar couldn't hear anything. He saw Zara, clutching her Cinderella purse. Her mouth was open, too. He knew she was howling. But again, no sound came out.

Then, suddenly, it came back with a roar! Omar heard Zara screaming, Dad shouting, and above it all, the *Car Talk* guys on NPR cackling about something called an Edsel. The only silent one was Mom. She lay on the floor with her mouth open, her eyes rolled up, not yelling, not groaning. She didn't even look like she was breathing.

That was when Omar began screaming himself. A very weird scream. It sounded as if he were standing across the room from himself, listening to himself yell. That was when he heard Dad shouting.

"Pull yourself together, Omar! I need your help!"

Omar's screaming stopped. He wanted to say, "Sure, Dad! Tell me what to do." But nothing came out. His mouth opened and closed like the mouth of a goldfish in an aquarium.

"Call 911!" he heard Dad say. "There!" Dad pointed across the kitchen to the phone on the wall. Somehow, Omar made it to the phone. Dad was on his knees beside Mom, holding her head and saying, "It'll be all right, Hoda. It'll be all right, Hoda," over and over again. Then Omar began to feel really scared, because Dad hardly ever called Mom by her first name unless something really, really bad happened.

Meanwhile, Zara had gotten down from her chair and was running around the kitchen in circles, screaming her head off. Neither Omar nor his dad had the time to pay any attention to her. Omar grabbed the phone. He had to think for a minute. "What's the number for 911?" Then his brain kicked in and things once again started making sense. He punched in the numbers.

A woman's voice on the other end of the line answered. "Nine-one-one Emergency. How may I help you?"

Omar shouted into the phone. He hoped the woman could hear him over Zara's howls. "My mom fell. She hit her head. She's not breathing."

"What's your address? We'll send an ambulance right away."

Address? Omar's mind went blank. He couldn't remember his own address.

"Three-nine-oh-eight South West Larch Drive. Wilsonville."

"Got it. Please stay on the line. Is there an adult I can speak to?"

"Yeah. My dad," Omar said.

"May I speak with him?"

"Who? Oh, Dad! Yeah. Sure."

Omar's dad held out his hand. Omar dashed across the room to give him the phone. "Thanks," Dad said. "Do something about Zara."

"Sure," said Omar. But before he could think of what to do about her, he heard sirens, followed by pounding on the door.

The ambulance was already there.

# chapter 21

A few minutes before, everything had appeared to be moving in slow motion. Now events zipped by at warp speed, as if someone had hit the Fast Forward button on the remote. Omar saw himself running to the front door. The next thing he knew, the kitchen and living room were full of firefighters and paramedics. Dad picked up Zara and handed her to Omar.

"Take her upstairs. She's just in the way," Dad said.

Omar felt Zara go limp in his arms. She kept moaning, "Mommy...Mommy..."

"Mom's gonna be okay," Omar heard himself saying as he started to carry Zara upstairs. He didn't know why he was saying that. He didn't know if Mom would be okay. All he knew was that the emergency squad had put some kind of plastic brace around her neck to hold her head steady. Then they'd put her on a gurney. Glancing over the banister, he saw the paramedics wheeling Mom out the door.

Just before Dad grabbed his coat and hurried after them, he called up to Omar, "I'm going to follow the ambulance. Keep your cell phone on. I'll call as soon as I know anything." And then he was gone. Omar heard the ambulance siren shrieking, the garage door opening, his dad driving away. Then silence.

A ticking clock.

A chattering radio.

Zara's soft sobs. "I want my mommy...."

Silence.

Omar carried Zara to her room. He cleared a space on her bed among the dolls and stuffed animals to lay her down. He sat next to her, rubbing her back, as she cried herself to sleep. "It's okay, Zara. Everything's gonna be okay. Mommy had to go to the doctor, but she'll be back. She'll be fine. It's gonna be okay."

Zara let out a deep sigh. Her thumb drifted to her mouth. Omar felt all her muscles relax. And then she was asleep. Omar tiptoed out of her room. He shut the door so quietly that it hardly made a click. He checked his pocket for his cell phone. It was on, and charged.

Now what? *Just wait, I guess,* Omar thought. *Wait for something to happen.*

He didn't have to wait long. He wasn't halfway downstairs when the front door opened and their neighbor Marianne walked in. Marianne was more than a neighbor. She was a good friend of his mom's. They went to an exercise class together twice a week. Marianne was an emergency room nurse. Her job was dealing with crises. She never thought twice about taking charge and ordering everybody else around.

Marianne had the key to the house. She'd let herself in the front door. "Omar, are you here?" she yelled. She was still wearing her scrubs, which meant that she'd just gotten back from her shift at the hospital.

"Zara's asleep," Omar called to her from the stairs.

"Good," Marianne said without missing a beat. "That's one less headache we have to deal with. Come down here so I can talk to you." Omar continued downstairs as Marianne kept on talking.

"I just spoke to your dad. He called me on the way to the

hospital. It's probably not a good idea to talk on the phone while you're following an ambulance. On the other hand, we don't have too many choices this morning, so we do what we have to do."

"Will my mom be all right?" Omar asked the question as Marianne paused for breath.

"Probably." Marianne said, taking a second to give him a reassuring pat before she was off again. "Your mom hit her head. She'll have a bad headache for a day or so. After that, she'll be okay. On the other hand, head trauma can be tricky. There might be a concussion, internal bleeding. You'll need to watch carefully over the next few days after your mom comes home."

"Watch for what?" Omar asked.

"You don't have to worry about that now. They'll go over it with your dad at the hospital. I'll be here, so you can always ask me if you have any questions." Marianne headed for the kitchen. Omar followed.

"Wow! What a mess!" Marianne said, looking over the wreckage of breakfast. "All that beautiful lox, too. What a waste! Okay, Omar. Let's get busy."

"Busy for what?" Omar said.

Marianne tapped on his forehead. "Hello in there! Is anybody home? Busy for what? Busy cleaning up this kitchen. I swear, is there some kind of disconnect attached to the male chromosome? Clue and less! Get a garbage bag and start picking up this mess from the floor. Where does your mom keep the bucket and the mop? What's this?"

Marianne lifted Zara's Cinderella purse from a sticky puddle of milk, orange juice, and cold coffee. She made a face. Marianne had grown up on a farm. Pink plastic princesses had never been her thing.

"It's Zara's," Omar said. "She has some kind of secret in it. She was showing it to Mom when—"

But Marianne was hardly listening. She opened the purse and looked inside. "Hey! There's hope for the kid yet," she said.

"Huh?" Omar said.

"Take a look." Marianne handed him the sticky, drippy purse. Omar didn't need more than a glimpse of red and orange to know what Zara's secret was.

"Arrow!" he said. The snake was curled tightly inside the right corner of Zara's Cinderella purse.

"I take it the critter's no stranger," Marianne said.

"He got out of his habitat. I've been looking for him for days," Omar said. He reached into the purse. Slowly, gently, he cupped his hand around Arrow. He felt the snake's cool, muscular body curling around his wrist. "Do snakes bother you?" he asked Marianne.

"Not a bit. I used to catch 'em and keep 'em as pets when I lived on Sauvie Island," Marianne said. "Good thing your mom isn't here. She hates the critters." Her eyes brightened, as if she'd suddenly caught on. "Or maybe your mom WAS here. Which is why I'm here and she's on her way to ER. Something like that?"

"Yeah," Omar said.

"Well, why don't you put your buddy back where he belongs? He'll probably be glad to get out of that plastic condo and into something a bit more environmentally friendly. I'll finish cleaning up here."

"Thanks, Marianne," Omar said as he headed upstairs to his bedroom.

"Don't mention it. What are neighbors for?"

Arrow remained coiled around Omar's arm all the way to the bedroom. He didn't attempt to glide from one arm to the other. He hardly moved at all. *He's done exploring,* Omar thought. Who could blame him? With all the noise and chaos of the morning's breakfast, not to mention being flipped in the air when the breakfast table went over—plus being cooped up for who knows how long in a kid's plastic purse manufactured out of Chinese toxic waste—what creature wouldn't look forward to a quiet, dark hide and a soft bed of aspen shavings?

"I'm starting to think like a snake," Omar said to himself. It wasn't hard to do.

Omar opened the habitat's lid. He rested his hand on the substrate. Arrow didn't move at first. He held on to Omar the way Zara had held on when Omar had carried her upstairs. Omar could imagine Arrow thinking: *I'm home now. My friend is here. He found me. I'm safe.*

"You're safe, Arrow," Omar said. It felt good to be able to say that after so many days of worrying. At the same time, Omar couldn't help feeling sad. Safe, yes. For a little while. And then Arrow would be gone. Arrow had put Mom in the hospital. No way his parents would let him keep a snake after that.

Omar waited for Arrow to uncoil. It took several minutes before the snake left Omar's arm and glided toward the substrate. Omar watched to see what he'd do. At first, he just glided around, his tongue flicking in and out, as if he were getting reacquainted with his home. Then he went over to the water dish. Omar saw the water's surface quiver as the snake drank. It seemed to take a long time, longer than Omar had ever seen Arrow drink.

*He's thirsty,* Omar thought. Arrow might not have had any water since Zara had shut him up in her purse. Not good. Snakes needed to drink every day. But if he'd been coming into Omar's room at night to drink, he might have been without water for only a couple of days. Anyhow, he seemed okay.

Omar wondered if Arrow was hungry. He made a quick calculation and decided that Arrow was due for another couple of pinkies. Should he give Samkatt a call to tell him to come over with the mice? He decided against it. He'd give Arrow a day or so to settle in. By then, he'd be on his way back to the Snake Dude.

Arrow finished drinking. He glided into his hide and disappeared. Omar knew better than to disturb him. He locked the habitat lid. No more escapes! He went down the hall to check on Zara. She was still asleep.

"Marianne?" Omar called, leaning over the banister. No answer. Marianne had let herself out when she finished. The kitchen looked like a hospital operating room. The floor was mopped, the garbage can emptied, the dishes stacked in the dishwasher. Everything was back in its place. The only thing left from the morning's disaster was the radio. Garrison Keillor was doing his joke show.

"I was walking downtown the other day when a homeless man came up to me and said, 'Hey, buddy, can you help me out? I haven't had a bite in days.'"

"So what did you do?"

"I bit him!"

It was the oldest, dumbest joke in the world. It was even dumber than the "jokes" Zara made up. Yet Omar couldn't help laughing. He laughed so hard he made his stomach ache as he repeated the punch line over and over again to himself.

"I bit him! I bit him! I bit him!"

# chapter 22

Dad called from the hospital a few hours later. All the news was good so far. The paramedics and the doctors couldn't find anything wrong with Mom other than a bad knock on the head. They were going to do a CT scan on her, just to make sure there were no internal injuries. Mom and Dad would have to wait a couple of hours for that, and then a couple more for the doctors to read the results.

"The ER's real crowded on weekends," Dad said. "If you're going to knock yourself out, best do it during the week. You won't have to wait as long."

Omar heard Mom's voice asking for the phone. "Omar, can you hear me?" She sounded woozy, as if she'd taken the kind of cough medicine that helps you sleep. "Everything's going to be okay, sweetie. I don't want you to worry. Marianne called Dad to tell him that you cleaned up the kitchen. Thanks for doing that, and for taking charge of Zara. How is she?"

"She's okay, Mom. She crashed as soon as I got her upstairs. I let her sleep as long as she wanted to. Then we watched videos." Endless videos. First *The Backyardigans*. Then *Wonder Pets*. Omar could hardly stand to watch them once. He couldn't understand how Zara could watch the same episode over and over again.

*And we're...your backyard friends, the Backyardigans...*

Omar thought about telling his mom how Zara had helped him refill Arrow's water dish with fresh water. Or how the two of them had sat in front of Arrow's habitat, waiting for him to come out of his hide. Arrow hadn't come out. And Omar didn't tell. Considering all that had happened, he didn't think Mom needed to hear about snakes.

Then it was time to wrap everything up, because the orderlies were coming to take Mom to the scanning room. "If we're not back by dinnertime, go over to Marianne's," Dad said. "Or there's plenty to eat in the refrigerator. You know what Zara likes." A quick "Goodbye. Love you." Then the line went dead.

Samkatt called. "Dude! What's going on at your house? I heard there were sirens and ambulances and the fire department came."

"My mom fell out of her chair this morning and hit her head. Knocked herself out cold. We were all scared. My dad just called from the hospital. She's gonna be okay."

"That's great, dude! Glad to hear it. I was worried. Want me to come over?"

"No, that's all right," Omar said. "I'm just looking after Zara till Mom and Dad get back from the hospital. Everything's cool."

"Smooth! Catch ya later."

"Yeah. Bye." As soon as he hung up, Omar realized that he hadn't told Samkatt about Arrow. And Samkatt hadn't asked. It was as if Arrow were gone already.

Or as if he had never been there at all.

Omar's parents came home at eight-thirty that evening. Omar had gotten Zara fed and into her pajamas. She wanted chicken nuggets and Cheerios for dinner, so that was what she got. By then Omar was convinced that processed food and the microwave were the two greatest inventions in the history of civilization. Mom looked pretty zonked when she came through the door. She said she could walk by herself, but it was obvious to Omar that Dad was holding her up. They helped Mom into the living room so she could sit down. Zara flung herself into Mom's lap. She went on and on about all the exciting things that had happened that day. She left out only one: Mom being carried off to the hospital in an ambulance.

Omar wondered about that. Had Zara forgotten? *How cool,* he thought, *to be able to take all the frightening memories and delete them.* But were they really deleted? Or did they remain permanently burned on the hard disk of your memory, overwritten thousands of times, but never completely erased? Wondering about that made Omar think he'd like to learn more about how the human mind worked. And computers.

Zara kept talking and clinging to Mom until Dad finally said, "Time for bed, princess!" Zara started crying as Dad carried her upstairs. She fell asleep before he'd gone halfway up.

Omar approached his mom's chair. "How are you, Mom?" he asked.

She took his hand and held it. "I'm fine. A knock on the head, that's all. I'm still not out of the woods. Dad has to wake me up every hour tonight and ask me dumb questions, like what year it is and what's my name."

"Why?" Omar asked.

"Just to make sure there's no bleeding inside my head. If I can't answer those questions, I go back to the hospital. Fast! Otherwise, I'm okay. I'll be my cranky old self once I get some sleep."

"You're not cranky, Mom," Omar said.

"Don't lie to me."

"Okay, maybe a little grumpy sometimes," Omar said.

"Give me a kiss!" Mom held tight to his hand as their lips touched. "Thanks for taking care of Zara. You really did a good job. I was worried that she might be upset or frightened. I asked

Dad to talk to Marianne about maybe coming over and taking charge. Marianne said you were doing fine and that you knew where to get help if you needed it. You're a very responsible boy, Omar. I'm glad I can count on you." She paused. "I'm sorry I made such a fuss about...your snake."

Omar felt his insides churning. Here was the moment. No point in dodging or running away. Mom was listening. Now was the time to tell her everything.

"My snake got loose," Omar began, his voice shaking. "I wanted to tell you. I talked about it with Dad. He offered to tell you first, but I wanted to do it. Then I lost my nerve. That's when Zara started talking about her secret. By then it was too late."

Mom listened quietly, not saying anything. She winced and closed her eyes tight, as if her head really hurt. She rubbed her forehead. It looked to Omar as if the pain eased. She opened her eyes again and said to Omar, "How did the snake get into Zara's purse?"

"Snakes need to hide," Omar said. He explained that a snake that had just eaten would naturally look for a hiding place to digest its meal. He told Mom how he'd really been looking for Arrow while he vacuumed the house. Samkatt's art lesson was a cover to keep her occupied while Omar searched.

"That rascal!" Omar's mom said.

"Don't blame him. He was just trying to help me," Omar said. "And he really did like the lesson. He learned a lot. He told me so. The one place I didn't have time to search was Zara's room. There was just too much stuff in there."

"Tell me about it," Mom said.

Omar laughed to himself. He was glad to know that—so far—his mom was following him. He continued. "I talked with Dad about what to do. He said it was best to come clean and admit Arrow got loose. We figured you'd have a fit and leave to go to the mall or somewhere. Then we'd have a chance to search Zara's room and the rest of the house if we couldn't find Arrow there."

"And what would happen if you did find him?"

"I'd take him back. That's what I'm going to do now. After you feel better and Dad can drive me to Portland." Omar's lips began to tremble. He tried his best to hold back. He couldn't. Something inside him broke and he found himself sobbing. He buried his face in Mom's lap.

"Mom... I'm so sorry. I never meant... I only wanted..."

Mom didn't answer. She didn't try to stop him. She let him cry, rubbing his back all the while, just as he had rubbed Zara's that morning until she fell asleep.

"It's okay," Mom finally whispered. "I'm not angry. You did nothing wrong. None of this is your fault."

Omar caught his breath. His eyes stung. He rubbed them with his wrist. "I'm sorry, Mom," he said again. "I'll give Arrow back. I never should have gotten a snake for a pet. I know how afraid of them you are."

Omar continued until he ran out of words and the breath to say them. Mom waited for him to finish.

"Arrow isn't going anywhere," she said. "I made up my mind. He stays."

"But you hate snakes!" Omar said.

"That's true. I hate them because I'm afraid of them. Which is something that has to change. I started thinking about this when I was in the hospital. I had a lot of time to think while I waited for the CT scan. Maybe what happened this morning wasn't all bad. Maybe I needed a smack on the head to bring me to my senses."

Omar began to worry that Mom might not be okay after all. Nothing she said made sense. "What do you mean, Mom?" he asked.

"Think about it," Mom said. "Arrow never left Zara's purse. He lets a four-year-old carry him around. You've handled him. Has he ever bitten you? Has he ever even hissed at you?"

"No," Omar said. "He's a pretty mellow snake. That's what the Snake Dude said when we got him."

147

"I believe it," Mom said. "So what knocked me out of my chair and into the wall? It wasn't Arrow. What was it?"

"I don't know," Omar said. Mom still wasn't making sense. She kept asking him questions like one of those TV judges, but the questions didn't seem to lead anywhere. Maybe something was going on in her brain? Omar wondered if he should call Dad. Maybe it was time to take her back to the hospital. He decided to give her a quick test, just to check her out.

"Uh, Mom," Omar said. "What's your name?"

"My name is Hoda Choufik-Kassar. Want me to spell it? I live in Wilsonville, Oregon. My husband's name is Ahmad. I have two children, Omar and Zara. Any more questions, Doctor?" She glared at Omar as if he'd brought a jumbo box of frozen mice into her living room.

"Sorry, Mom," Omar said. "The way you were talking had me worried. You weren't making sense."

Her face softened. "Maybe I was coming on too strong. Thanks for being concerned. But you don't have to worry. There's nothing wrong with my brain. At least, nothing that can't be fixed. You see, Omar, your little snake Arrow didn't knock me against the wall and send me to the hospital. Fear did it. My own fear of snakes. So you might say I did it to myself."

"I guess," Omar said, trying his best to follow her thoughts.

"I did. No question about it," Mom continued. "So while I was lying on the gurney in the hospital, I started thinking back to when I was a little girl in Beirut. We lived with fear in a way you can't imagine. Shootings, bombings, bodies lying in the street. It went on day and night without letup. People you knew would be murdered—your best friend's dad, your teacher, the man who owned the toy store, the couple who ran the falafel stand. Nobody knew who did it, or why. When you live with fear like that, it becomes part of you. Then fear leads to hate. Soon everybody hates everybody else. Muslims hate Christians; Christians hate Muslims. And different kinds of Christians and Muslims hate different kinds of Muslims and Christians. It never ends. Hate and fear feed each other.

"My father—your grandpa—was a remarkable man. He refused to allow his children to grow up hating and fearing their neighbors. So we left. First to France, then to America. Can you believe we were here six months before I would go out of the house by myself? I was afraid someone would kill me. I cried every time my dad left for work. I thought I might never see him again."

Omar didn't say anything. He just listened. He'd never known his grandpa. His mom had never really spoken much about what it was like to live in Lebanon during the country's civil war. Or as Dad sometimes said, "ONE of their civil wars." The way Mom talked about it now made it sound like living in one of Samkatt's cartoons, where everyone was killing everyone else. Except there were no samurai cat superheroes coming to save the day.

"What does that have to do with being afraid of snakes?" Omar asked. "I don't get it."

"Neither did I," Mom said. "Then today, at the hospital, I suddenly figured it out. One night, when we were still living in Lebanon, these militiamen came to our house. No, 'came' isn't the word. They kicked down the door. They dragged my father into the kitchen and shoved everyone else into one of the bed-rooms. Two of them kept us under guard while the others questioned Daddy. Questioned? That's a joke! They beat him up. We could hear it in the bedroom. I remember I tried to cover my ears with my hands so I wouldn't have to listen, but I could still hear Daddy's cries as those thugs worked him over."

Omar listened quietly. He'd never heard this story before.

"You don't know what terror is like until you go through something like that," Mom said. "These guys meant business. Who knew what they wanted or what they might do? They could have kidnapped Daddy. Or killed him. They could have killed us all, too. The entire family. The two guys who were guarding us kept their AK-47s pointed at us the whole time.

"Then suddenly I remembered. One of those guys—those awful militiamen with their masks and guns who were tearing up our home and screaming at us and threatening us—one of those guys had a tattoo on his arm."

"A tattoo?" Omar asked.

"A tattoo of a snake," Mom said.

"You're afraid of snakes...because some guy in Lebanon had a tattoo? That doesn't make sense, Mom," Omar said.

"Fear doesn't have to make sense, Omar," Mom said. "It's like catching a disease. One tiny microbe enters your system. It grows and multiplies until it takes over your body. Fear works the same way, except it takes over your mind. That thug in Lebanon with his stupid tattoo infected me with a fear of snakes. Look where it led."

"Where?" Omar still wasn't sure he was catching on.

Mom gripped Omar's hands between hers. She stared into his eyes. "Can't you see? Remember how I yelled at you for bringing dead mice into the house? I brought in something much worse than mice. Fear—unreasoning fear of a harmless little animal that can't possibly hurt anyone. I have to do something about it before it infects my children. Today you're afraid of snakes. Tomorrow you're afraid of people. And what you fear, you hate. Where does it end? It ends now. And to end it, I need a snake, so I can look at the snake and maybe touch it and hold it without being afraid. So I can finally get the memory of that awful night in Lebanon out of my house, out of my mind, out of my life."

"I get it, Mom," Omar said. "I want a snake. You NEED a snake."

"Exactly!" She went on, "And then there's that painting I'm working on."

"The one in your studio?" Omar said.

"Yeah, that's right," Mom said. "I'm on to something there.

This could be an important piece. Maybe a real breakthrough for me and my art. But it's not working because the snake isn't right. It looks like a painted rope, a rubber snake. The snake has to come alive for the picture to work. But I can only bring it to life if I know snakes. I have to know what they look like, feel like. How their bodies are put together. I have to feel the muscles beneath the skin. I have to look into their eyes without turning away. I can't do any of that if I'm afraid of snakes."

"I can help you, Mom," Omar said. "Would you like me to bring Arrow down so you can hold him?"

Omar saw his mom flinch. "Uh...not tonight, sweetie. Mommy's tired. Can we save Arrow for tomorrow?"

"Sure, Mom," Omar said. At the same time, he couldn't help thinking, *So this is what it must be like to shed your skin. To shed your old habits, your fears. To bust out of that too-tight, worn-out wrapper that's holding you in and leave it all behind. You begin again. You create a new you.*

"I'm starting to think like a snake," Omar murmured to himself later that evening as he watched Arrow gliding around his habitat. Which wasn't bad. After all, snakes must know something. They've only been around for a hundred million years.

# Author's Note

This book began as a story about a boy who wanted a pet snake, mostly because I wanted a pet snake and writing about one would give me an excuse to get one of my own. It grew into something more.

Special thanks are due to Dr. Michael S. Klaybor for helping me understand how phobias work. Thanks are also due to Blake Oren, A. J. Hooper, Marianne Lynde, Walter Mayes, Ali Karni, Sami Haydar, Noran Ameer, Loreen Leedy, Mohammed and Fatima Hariry, Steve Borsuk, Ibrahim Abunayyan, Brenda Rockwood, and Mina Javaherbin for sharing their knowledge and insights. Finally, although he doesn't realize it, I owe a debt to Pirate, my corn snake, who is endlessly forgiving and patient, even when I'm late in delivering his mouse.

Dad's story about Daadi Samp is fictional, but it is based on fact. The government of Pakistan is making great efforts to educate people about the ecological and economic value of snakes. The number of people who die from snakebite is a tiny fraction of the number killed by diseases carried by mice and rats.

Snakes don't hunt humans. They bite only when they feel threatened or trapped. If you encounter a snake in the wild, remain quiet and calm. Back off. Give the snake plenty of room. It will move away from you as quickly as it can.

Some people are deathly afraid of snakes. This fear should be respected. No one who is afraid of snakes should ever be teased or bullied with a live snake. It is bad for the person and bad for the snake.

Keeping a pet snake is a good way to overcome the irrational fears and prejudices people have about these fascinating creatures. Snakes make excellent pets for those who are willing to make the effort to learn about them and provide for their needs. It's a major commitment. A pet corn snake can live as long as twenty years. If the idea of keeping a snake interests you, there are numerous online sites, forums, and videos to help you learn more.